Hoop Crazy

BOOKS BY

CLAIR BEE

TECHNICAL

The CLAIR BEE *Basketball Library*
1. The Science of Coaching
2. Fundamentals and Drills
3. Man-to-Man Defense and Attack
4. Zone Defense and Attack

The JUNIOR ALL-AMERICAN *Sports Library*
1. Football
2. Basketball
3. Baseball

CLAIR BEE's Basketball Quiz Book
The Beginning Basketball Coach
One Hundred Basketball Shots
Great Basketball Thrills by Basketball **Greats**
CLAIR BEE's Basketball Annual
Winning Basketball Plays by America's
    Greatest Coaches
The Basketball Player's Handbook
The Jumbo Book of Basketball
Basketball
The Basketball Coach's Notebook

FICTION

The CHIP HILTON *Sports Stories*

Touchdown Pass	A Pass and a Prayer
Championship Ball	Dugout Jinx
Strike Three!	Freshman Quarterback
Clutch Hitter!	Backboard Fever
Hoop Crazy	Fence Busters
Pitchers' Duel	Ten Seconds to Play!
Fourth Down Showdown	

For a second it looked as though he might be trapped

For a second it looked as though he might be trapped

Hoop Crazy

A CHIP HILTON SPORTS STORY

Hoop Crazy

BY CLAIR BEE

GROSSET & DUNLAP   Publishers   New York

TO

WILLIAM "DOLLY" KING

Student, athlete, gentleman,

and friend

Contents

CONTENTS

CHAPTER 1

HOOP CRAZY

THE TALL, blond forward in the red-and-white suit feinted toward the basket and then broke out toward the backcourt where a teammate with powerful legs and broad shoulders was holding the ball. Leaping high in the air, the lithe forward took the pass and landed as easily as a cat in front of the free-throw line. The stocky forward followed the pass and cut by the blond boy with a sudden burst of speed. The towhead faked a pass to the flying figure, pivoted suddenly and dribbled toward the basket. There was a sudden converging of the orange-clad opponents on the blond youngster and for a second it looked as though he might be trapped. But just as his opponents seemed to have him surrounded and bottled up, the rangy forward leaped high in the air and hooked a fast, accurate pass directly into the hands of the tallest of his teammates who was standing unguarded under the basket, and the big 14 registered on the home team side of the scoreboard flashed to 16.

It was a beautiful play and the continuous roar of cheers testified to the home town rooters' appreciation. Halfway up the bleachers and smack in the middle of the wild Valley Falls High School cheering section, a tall, important-looking man with a small mustache had been impassively watching the game. The very fact that he had not joined in the cheering stamped him as a stranger in town. With the possible exception of the newcomer, there wasn't a person in the building who wasn't excitedly following every play in the tense contest between the Big Reds of Valley Falls and the Salem Sailors. The din was terrific and the stranger breathed a sigh of relief when the Salem captain called "Time!" and the noise subsided momentarily.

But the sheer beauty of the play he had just witnessed seemed to be too much even for the stranger. He elbowed the excited man next to him and asked, "Who is that kid?"

There seemed to be no doubt in the mind of the man he addressed whom the stranger meant. "Him?" he said enthusiastically, nodding in the general direction of the court. "That kid? Why, he's the best basketball player in the state! That's young Hilton! Chip Hilton!"

"Yeah," a man on the other side added, "and the leading scorer in the state, too!"

The stranger gravely thanked his informants and would have withdrawn into his shell, but it was too late now. He had started something and they meant to finish it. He got information from all sides and no quarter.

"Averaging more than twenty points a game, so far—"

"Yeah, had ninety-eight up to tonight! Ain't bad, heh?"

"Got twenty-nine in the first game! The all time record is thirty-nine—"

"Comes by it natural! His dad set the record years ago."

"Yeah, there was a big write-up in the papers coupla nights ago about it. Didn't you see it?"

The stranger assured them he hadn't read the paper, except for the news about the big pottery exhibit. That was the reason for his presence in Valley Falls. . . . Oh, sure he liked basketball. . . . No, he hadn't known Valley Falls was the state champion. . . . Yes, it sure was something that a little town like Valley Falls could be defending champions of such a big state. . . . Yes, that Hilton kid was terrific. Yes, he could see that Ch— What was his name? Chip? That Chip Hilton was a team player as well as a scorer. . . . Yes, he knew Chip was the captain—

The dashing return of the home team to the floor and the explosion which greeted them saved him. Play was resumed and the stranger was forgotten by the Big Red rooters who surrounded him. Down on the court, William "Chip" Hilton, the focal point of every rabid fan's interest, continued to dominate the game.

With the resumption of play, the stranger leaned back against the restless knees of the woman directly behind him and concentrated on the Hilton boy. He appreciated know-how in any form and the basketball savvy of this kid was beautiful to watch. He had realized that this town was keenly interested in basketball when he had arrived that morning. Printed and hand-painted game signs were everywhere, in the depot, in the modest hotel where he had registered, in the shop-windows and on the telephone poles. After he had el-bowed and fought his way through the entrance and into the packed high school gym and had sat through the first five minutes of the hectic struggle, there no longer was any doubt in his mind that every resident of the town of Valley Falls was hoop crazy.

The tall stranger liked basketball. Not too many years ago he had been a pretty fair basketball shot himself. In fact, he still was an expert marksman. Shooting a basketball is something like riding a bicycle or swimming. Once a fellow learns to shoot a basketball, ride a bicycle, or swim, he never loses his skill. The man with the graying mustache had never entirely given up shooting a basketball. He had stuck to his hobby because a fellow didn't need company when it came to shooting a basketball. Especially when he never stops long enough in one place to develop friends. For years, in his travels about the country, he had enjoyed dropping into the local Y's and practicing his shots. It never took him long to get an audience. If there was one thing he had learned well when he was a youngster it had been how to shoot a basketball. Especially accurate was his long one-hand shot. Sitting there in the grandstand, he could almost fancy himself in the yellow-thatched kid's shoes. The kid wasn't bad . . . even with two hands.

When the half ended, Valley Falls was leading, 20 to 14, and the newcomer again became the target of an informatory barrage about the Big Reds and Chip Hilton. He learned that Henry "the Rock" Rockwell, Valley Falls' veteran mentor, was the best coach in the state, and that Chip Hilton and the speedy youngster with the rugged build both were three-sport lettermen. The man on the right fished a crumpled schedule out of his pocket and carefully wrote in the scores of the games which Valley Falls had played to date.

"We won 'em all so far and we're almost a cinch to win all the rest of 'em. The games with the little stars in front of 'em are the teams we gotta beat to win our section. We won't have any trouble doin' that, brother. We're a cinch to repeat in the section and in the state, too. You'll see us up in the finals all right! Here, stick this schedule in your pocket and watch our smoke!"

The stranger put on a show of studying the schedule because it gave him a little relief from the red-hot basketball chatter of his new-found friends. He didn't know much about the teams, but it was easy to see that the Big Reds had gotten off to a good start.

VALLEY FALLS HIGH SCHOOL

Basketball Schedule

Fri.	Nov.	29	Alumni	Home	61–47
Sat.	”	30	Clinton	Home	48–22
Fri.	Dec.	6	New Benton	Away	47–39
Sat.	”	7	West Haven	Away	38–34
* Fri.	”	13	Salem	Home	
* Sat.	”	14	Delford	Home	
* Fri.	”	20	Dane	Away	
* Sat.	”	28	Stratford	Home	
* Fri.	Jan.	3	Dulane	Home	
* Fri.	”	10	Southern	Away	
* Fri.	”	17	Parkton	Home	
* Wed.	”	22	Weston	Away	
* Wed.	”	29	Steeltown	Home	
* Fri.	”	31	Northville	Away	
* Fri.	Feb.	7	Hampton	Home	
* Fri.	”	14	Southern	Home	
* Fri.	”	21	Steeltown	Away	
* Fri.	”	28	Delford	Away	

* Section Two

State Tournament: March 5, 7, 8 (State University)

Last Year's Sectional Champs and Runner-ups

North (Sec. 1)	South (Sec. 2)	East (Sec. 3)	West (Sec. 4)
Waterbury	Weston	Bloomfield	Rutledge
Coreyville	Valley Falls	Edgemont	Seaburg

STATE CHAMPIONS: VALLEY FALLS
RUNNERS-UP: RUTLEDGE

The second half was almost a repetition of the first. Chip Hilton and the hard-driving guard, Robert "Speed" Morris, seemed to be confusing the Salem defense. The speedster would pass the ball to Hilton, follow the pass by cutting to the right or the left of the rangy ball handler, and attempt to drive his opponent into the block set up by the big forward. If Morris succeeded in picking off his opponent on the block which Hilton would set up, Chip would give the ball back to his hard-cutting teammate who would be free for a shot at the basket. If the man guarding Hilton switched to pick up the speeding guard, Hilton would pivot and shoot or dribble in for an easy lay-up.

The stranger shook his head in admiration of the play of these two boys. It was apparent that they had practiced their two-man plays hundreds of times. Oblivious now to the frenzied cheering of the home town rooters who surrounded him, the stranger began to think of his own days as a basketball player and then of his present predicament. He had come to the game tonight because of his love for basketball and because it was an inexpensive way to spend an evening. Tomorrow he'd have to get out to that pottery convention and figure out an angle to raise some quick cash. He sighed and turned his attention back to the floor.

Even with Chip and Speed's smooth teamwork the game was no walkaway, and the Salem Sailors fought hard. But the poise and experience of the Big Reds were too much for their opponents and the game ended with Valley Falls chalking up its fifth straight victory, 37 to 31. On the way out of the gym, through the trophy foyer and down the long steps to the street, the tall stranger's enthusiastic seatmate kept up a steady flow of conversation about the game, Chip Hilton, Speed Morris, the Rock, Taps Browning, the towering junior center, Soapy

Smith and Buzz Todd, the set-shot deadeyes, Red Schwartz, Speed Morris' backcourt running mate, and even Biggie Cohen, the six-foot four-inch student manager, also about J. P. Ohlsen, the big pottery man who had given the gym to the town.

"So you're a pottery man, too? Well, you've got plenty of company as long as you're in this town. That's about the only industry in Valley Falls and about everyone here has worked there one time or another. J. P. believes in helping the townfolks. Great guy—J. P. Don't miss the exhibit out there tomorrow. You'll see Chip Hilton, too. He's got an exhibit, believe it or not! Not his own stuff, but some ware his old man made years ago. Kid's father is dead, you know. Got killed in the pottery, saving some guy's life. Big Chip—everybody called him Big Chip—was the chief chemist for Ohlsen. Was good, too! Graduate of State and knew his stuff.

"You know, we didn't have Hilton last year. Hurt his leg in football or some way and didn't play. Managed the team, though. That's why we're a cinch to repeat! We've got everybody back from last year plus Hilton! It's a cinch! Well, got to turn off here. Hope you're going to be in town for the game tomorrow night. Better get over here early if you want to get a seat. Playing Delford! Tough team! Tough coach, too! It'll be a knock 'em down and drag 'em out game. Guy by the name of Jenkins is Delford's coach. Hates the Rock! Everybody calls Rockwell the Rock. He's our coach, you know. Well, so long once again. Hope to see you tomorrow night."

The stranger said good night and mentally resolved that the Valley Falls gym was one place where he wouldn't be found tomorrow night or any other night if he could help it. As he continued along with the crowd, listening to their loud and excited voices, he shook his head in disbelief. Then someone asked how many points Chip Hilton had made and it seemed to the stranger that fifty voices answered "Twenty-two!"

"Yeah, nine buckets! That's all, just nine!"

"And four charity tosses!"

"That gives him a hundred and twenty for five!"

"Wait and see what he gets tomorrow night," someone bantered. "Jenkins'll have two men on him!"

"He'll need five to stop Chip!"

The stranger turned off that street at the next corner. "It's a mania with these people," he muttered half-aloud. "They're hoop crazy!"

CHAPTER 2

STRANGER IN TOWN

THE SUGAR BOWL was jammed with the after-game crowd and Petey Jackson, Valley Falls' champ soda jerk, was busily engaged in filling the never-ending stream of orders for double-frosteds, cokes, Big Red specials, sundaes, and banana splits. Busy as Petey was, however, he had time to keep a weather eye on his star assistant, the one and only Soapy Smith.

"I'm indispensable," Soapy gravely informed Speed Morris as he crammed a third dipper of ice cream into the tall glass, "indispensable, Speed, that's all! There, try that on your diaphragm!"

Petey tapped Soapy on the shoulder. "You basketball guys are s'posed to be in training—right?"

Soapy regarded Petey solemnly. "Right!" he agreed.

"Then cut out influencing athletes to break training!"

Soapy turned away from Petey and gazed around the crowded fountain incredulously. "Did you hear that?" he managed. "Influencing athletes! Me! How about them influencing me? I'm a athlete, ain't I?"

Petey regarded him with a withering glance. "Someone's been propergandering you. You ain't even on the team!"

9

Soapy was offended. "What am I doin' on the bench then, if I ain't on the team?" he wanted to know.

"Taking up room that belongs to the water boy!"

The laughter which followed Petey's remark didn't seem to worry Soapy. "Okay, then I'm a water boy! At least I'm carrying water for the best team in the state!"

That brought a cheer from the whole crowd. Chip Hilton, back in the storeroom where he spent most of his time packing and unpacking the goods for the drugstore next door as well as the Sugar Bowl, poked his head out to learn the reason for the uproar.

Soapy spied him. "There's Chip," he cried. "Ask him if I ain't on the team!"

Biggie Cohen, the basketball manager, wheeled around on the tiny chair which was completely hidden under his two hundred and thirty pounds. "Hey, Chip," he called, "come here and take care of Soapy."

Chip sauntered up to the fountain and was soon caught in the middle of Petey and Soapy's argument. In the meantime, the high school customers waited impatiently, facetiously voicing their opinions of the help at the Sugar Bowl and threatening to take their business elsewhere. But the threats had no effect on the three employees who depended upon the Sugar Bowl for their livelihood. Petey was a full-time employee while Chip Hilton and Soapy Smith worked part time. Chip had worked for the kindly owner of the drugstore for several years, but Soapy was comparatively new on the job. Soapy had taken Chip's place the past summer while Chip was working in Mansfield and John Schroeder had kept him on after Chip's return.

The three friends faced one another now, arguing heatedly to the delight of the interested customers who began to order recklessly, secure in the knowledge that they wouldn't be served even if their demands did register.

"Where's my Valley Falls delight?"

"How about four banana splits?"

"Gimme three more double-frosteds!"

"*Please*, may I have a coke, you jerks!"

The discussion and the uproar might have continued until closing time had not John Schroeder and old Doc Jones sauntered in after a leisurely walk following the game. In a second, three youngsters in white coats were falling all over one another, each trying to fill the same order. But Doc Jones and John Schroeder appeared not to notice anything unusual and continued on through the crowd to the storeroom.

At eleven thirty, Chip, Soapy, and Biggie Cohen started home. Waiting for them at the street door were Taps Browning and Speed Morris.

"Another minute and you'd have had to walk home," Speed chided. "Don't you guys ever quit?"

"Yes," added Taps, shivering, "remember the time of the year. This isn't July, you know."

Speed waved a hand grandiloquently to Taps Browning. "Open the door for the gentlemen, Taps."

Browning bent his six-foot six-inch frame nearly to the ground in a deep bow and pretended to open an imaginary door on Speed's jalopy. The battered car was doorless and practically fenderless. But it ran and so the manager and four important members of Valley Falls' "wonder team" went chugging home.

The basketball hopes of Valley Falls rode in that overloaded car. Chip Hilton, the Big Red captain and high scorer, was a tall, lanky kid who tilted the beam for a hard one hundred and eighty pounds.

Hilton's chief running mate was the owner-driver of

the car, Speed Morris. Morris was a chunky five-tenner with speed to burn. He hit one hundred and seventy pounds stripped, moved as if jet-propelled, and was the spark plug of the hoop squad. A hard dribbler and a good passer, Speed was the backcourt quarterback who started most of the plays on the offense and was responsible for the defensive balance of the team.

The shorty of the group, redheaded, freckled-faced Soapy Smith was five feet eight and inclined to be chunky. But he wasn't slow and he wasn't lazy and he was a good basketball player with a splendid set shot. Soapy was ambitious some of the time, happy most of the time, irrepressible all of the time.

Taps Browning, Chip Hilton's elongated shadow was six feet six inches in height, extremely slender, and Valley Falls' star center. Although he weighed only one hundred and seventy pounds, his frame was large and he was beginning to show signs of filling out. Taps was the youngest boy in the crowd and the only one who would not be graduated the following June.

The last, but certainly not the least, was two hundred and thirty pounds of athletic muscle. Bernie "Biggie" Cohen had been the anchor man of the Big Red football and baseball teams ever since he entered Valley Falls High School. Besides that, he had played baseball for three years, in the outfield the first year and then replacing Hilton at first base when Chip had been first made into a catcher and then changed to a pitcher. Cohen threw lefty and was a southpaw power hitter.

Hilton and Morris had been three-letter men ever since their first year in high school and had tried to get Biggie on that list by encouraging him to play basketball. But the round ball didn't have enough handles for Biggie and he had given up in disgust. Hilton and Morris hadn't given up, though, and had finally achieved their goal by having Coach Rockwell appoint Cohen manager of the hoop team.

Speed Morris was proud of his ancient jalopy. Not because it was underslung, souped-up, and painted a brilliant red and white, but because it was as faithful as a doting mother, never failed to carry the mail, and was always raring to go. The four-lunger's muffler had rusted off years ago and the loud explosions which accompanied the bumpy progress of the chariot were ear-splitting. The conversation of the passengers was, of necessity, carried on by means of shouts and bellows.

"Guess we doused the Sailors, all right," Soapy Smith hollered.

Taps Browning cupped a hand to his mouth and yelled happily, "Number five for the record!"

Biggie Cohen shook his fist under Soapy's nose. "And thirteen to go," he roared, "thirteen!"

A few minutes later Speed expertly braked the jitterbug into the curbstone in front of the Hilton home. The noisy passengers piled out and barged up the walk, onto the porch, through the unlocked door, and into a big, comfortably furnished living room where Chip's mother was reading a book. The noisy intrusion brought no look of surprise to Mrs. Hilton's face. She was used to these sudden visits by Chip's friends. In fact, she looked forward to meeting these boys as eagerly as they looked forward to meeting her. The Hilton home, long the center of activities for a group of athletic-minded high school youngsters, was always open to Chip's friends.

Sunday dinners and after-game snacks provided Mrs. Hilton with one of her greatest pleasures. She enjoyed having Chip and his companions in the house. Tonight, her smiling gray eyes were joyfully proud as she kissed her son and patted him on the shoulder.

"You were splendid tonight, Chip," she said happily, "splendid!"

"I'll say he was," Biggie said admiringly. "Twenty-two points!"

"And he should've had more," Speed growled. "Heck, he passes off too much. We have to fight with him to get him to shoot."

"Yeah," Soapy grumbled, "he acts like he ain't s'posed to shoot! Why, his shootin' average is better'n forty per cent! The rest of us can't hit better'n one out of four! Hey, what's on the menu?"

Without waiting for an answer, Soapy bolted from the room with Taps right behind him. The others followed, but before they reached the kitchen, Soapy was bellowing:

"What's this? What goes here? We gonna eat off Indian pottery?"

It looked that way. The kitchen table was loaded down with clay bowls, plates, and vases of all sizes and colors.

"What's that all about?" Speed asked.

Mrs. Hilton laughed. "Why, that's Chip's idea," she said. "That's the ware he's going to exhibit tomorrow at the pottery convention."

"You mean sell, Mother," Chip said, "at least try to sell—"

While the others had been talking, Biggie Cohen had been examining several of the pieces of ware, carefully estimating the weight, the finish, and the texture of the clay. Now he nodded approvingly:

"Gee, that's nice stuff, Chip. You didn't—"

Chip checked him, shaking his head vigorously and exchanging glances with his mother.

"Chip's father made it years ago," Mrs. Hilton explained. "It's been up in the attic all that time and Chip thought perhaps he could sell it and the money could be added to his college fund."

"Not all of it, Mother," Chip corrected. "I'm going to keep some of the best pieces. I've got them down in the lab in the cellar." He paused and forced a little laugh before continuing. "Maybe I can get forty or fifty dollars for it. Every dollar helps, you know."

Chip laughed lightly again. But inside he wasn't laughing. That college fund was serious and it wouldn't be long until he'd be needing money for board and room and his other college bills. Eight months fly by pretty fast.

"Look," Soapy said aggrievedly, "I didn't come here to talk!"

Mary Hilton took care of that without further delay.

Valley Falls was a small town with but one chief industry, the pottery. There wasn't much need for a hotel, but there were two to choose from and, at any other time, you would have had little trouble getting a room. But it was different tonight because Valley Falls was filled with visitors who were in town for the pottery convention and exhibit.

After the tall newcomer had left the basketball crowd, he made a tour of Main Street from one end to the other before returning to his hotel. Then he sat in the lobby listening to the talk of the visiting pottery men and trying to figure a way out of his financial predicament. He had a strong hunch that things were going to break for him in this burg! A little later he made his way to the room which had been assigned to him, locked the door carefully, and inspected the transom and the window looking out over the first-floor porch.

He placed a key ring, knife, watch, and a slim roll of bills on the bed table and slowly removed his clothes. Then he snapped off the light and, sitting there on the side of the bed in the darkness, slipped the watch and the roll of bills in the toe of one of his socks and tucked it under his pillow. He hefted the key ring and felt of the odd assortment of keys which were attached to it. He smiled grimly as he jingled them softly. They were about as important as money . . . in his business.

He reached under the pillow and placed the keys in the sock and slipped the sock back under the pillow before climbing into bed. You couldn't tell about small-town hotels and that thin roll of bills represented all the money in the world to him right now. He had seen the day when the roll he carried was a big fat one. But things had been tough lately and the money was slipping away like water. Well, he'd think of something tomorrow. He'd have to think of something pretty soon.

The stranger was a pottery man of sorts and had been around potteries all his life. Mostly, however, he lived by his wits. He had come to Valley Falls to try to wrangle an angle out of the convention and exhibit. His thoughts drifted back to the basketball game and the big, blond kid. That disturbed him, thinking about basketball and basketball players when he should be thinking about an angle to raise money.

He'd been a pretty fair country basketball player himself not too long ago. He hadn't been much of a team man then, and he wasn't much of a team man now. He'd rather go his way alone. Funny about basketball, though. He had always been a crack shot. He clasped the long fingers of his soft hands together. Guess he couldn't do much with those hands except shoot baskets or manipulate locks. He chuckled in the dark. Well, it was a lot easier to let the other fellow do the work. Why get calloused when you can use your noggin? He'd better get busy, though, or he might have to go to work, after all.

Early breakfasts were the rule at the Hilton home and Chip was up at six o'clock, making last-minute preparations for his exhibit. Mary Hilton's duties as supervisor of the local telephone exchange did not require her presence until eight o'clock and Chip was not expected at the Sugar Bowl and drugstore until seven thirty, but breakfast was always ready at seven o'clock. Chip could make it down to the Sugar Bowl in ten minutes and by eight thirty on school days he had his work finished. Today he wanted to get away early so he could get his ware down to the pottery recreation center in plenty of time. He hurried through his breakfast and then hustled down to the Sugar Bowl. By seven thirty he had everything shipshape.

The recreation hall at the pottery recreation center was bustling with activity when Chip arrived, and he was soon busy arranging the ware he had brought on the little stand Abe Cohen, Biggie Cohen's brother, had assigned him. The doors opened at nine o'clock sharp and it seemed to Chip that every person in Valley Falls and in the state, too, was there. Chip's ware didn't last long. He sold all but two of the odd pieces in the exhibit before eleven o'clock. The eagerness of the men to buy his pieces almost tempted him to go home and get a few more, but he put that thought out of mind. He had determined to keep those beautiful examples of his father's handicraft and they were now safe under lock and key in the small lab Big Chip had built in the cellar and there they were going to stay.

The tall stranger arrived early, too. He whistled in

admiration when he saw the building J. P. Ohlsen had built for his employees. J. P. Ohlsen had really splurged when he built this recreation building. In addition to a splendid cafeteria, library, exercise rooms of all kinds, bowling alleys, billiard rooms, reading rooms, and a small theater, the building boasted a fine gym and a large dance floor. The exhibit was being held on the dance floor.

After the newcomer had inspected the building, he wandered from booth to booth examining the ware. He covered the room thoroughly, covertly studying the men who were there, appraising them shrewdly, and cataloging each in his mind. He contrived to be busily engaged in examining a piece of ware close to whatever group of men were talking pottery. One group interested him particularly. The men were older, obviously prosperous, and their talk stamped them as experts in ceramics. He moved closer and listened intently as they minutely examined a small piece of ware.

"It's beautiful," one of the men said approvingly.

"I haven't seen anything like that for a long, long time. Where'd you get it?"

"From the tall, blond kid over at that little table. Said his father made it years ago in his home lab."

"You never see that kind of stuff any more. Can't get the clay!"

"Nor the chemists, either."

"You've got something there!"

"I guess Ohlsen would give a pretty penny to pick up some clay and a formula or two which could turn out that kind of ware."

"You're not far wrong there! He's going to have to do something and do it quick. He isn't getting the kind of clay he wants from England now, and I understand he's planning to try something new next year. Got his chemists working overtime on domestic clays and new formulas."

"There he is now, talking to the kid who sold me this."

The stranger replaced the piece of ware he had been examining so intently while he listened to the conversation of the out-of-town potters, and sauntered away. As he moved along from table to table and in the direction of Chip's table, he carefully appraised the tall man who was sponsoring this exhibit and who was so prominent in the field of ceramics. Then, as if struck by a sudden thought, he stopped abruptly and snapped his fingers. His eyes narrowed and his face was lighted by a grim smile. This was the angle! Ohlsen was the ticket . . . wealthy . . . desperate for a new formula or a source of clay . . . ripe for plucking. . . . Why fool around with two-for-a-nickel stuff when you can land something big?

J. P. Ohlsen was a friendly man. Tall, lanky of body, he carried himself with the poise and assurance which bespeaks confidence and strength. His stern face gave you the impression of a cold nature at first meeting, but after a short time you knew him to be a good man who believed in fair play in business as well as in sports. He was in a hurry, now, but he took time to stop by Chip's display for a friendly word. J. P. Ohlsen liked Chip Hilton. He liked the spirit and the ambition which this tall, good-looking kid with the level, gray eyes displayed in his work, his studies, and in his play.

"Looks as though you're pretty well sold out, Chip," he said with a chuckle. "Is that all you have left?"

"No, sir," Chip said quickly, "I've got some more that Dad made at home. But I'm not going to sell that! I'm working with some of Dad's old formulas and trying to make a few pieces myself."

Ohlsen's eyes lighted with pleasure. "You mean your dad's lab in the cellar is still there?"

"Yes, sir! Still working, too. Of course, I'm not very good and I have a lot of trouble figuring out the formulas Dad had worked up, but I have a lot of fun trying."

Ohlsen was nodding his head as Chip talked, but his thoughts were far away. Absent-mindedly he wished Chip good luck and walked away. He was thinking of another Hilton, the Hilton who had been his chief chemist and who had lost his life trying to save the life of a careless workman when this youngster was just a little boy. Life moved fast. He could go back over the years when Bill Hilton had come back to Valley Falls with his sheepskin and a head full of great ideas about pottery and clay and formulas. Bill had moved fast, too —right up to chief chemist. Ohlsen's face tightened up a bit as he thought of the fine work Hilton had done and the progress the plant had made in those early days. He needed a Bill Hilton now.

The tall stranger had maneuvered so that he overheard the entire conversation between Chip and J. P. Ohlsen. When Ohlsen left, the newcomer made his way toward the exit. He was all set now. The plan which had been rapidly taking form in his agile mind was practically complete and the first step was clear. The Valley Falls coup depended to a great extent upon making the acquaintance of Chip Hilton and getting a peek at that laboratory and those formulas which were in the basement of the Hilton home.

CHAPTER 3

A BATTLE OF WITS

THE VALLEY FALLS Public Library was small, but it carried in its archives just about everything that had ever happened in the town or to one of its citizens. A tall, spare man with a graying mustache lost no time in securing permission to use the newspaper files in the library stocks. He concentrated on the *Times* and the *Post* in the "twenty-years-ago" period. He spent the entire afternoon and evening making notes that were concerned with the life and times of "Big Chip" Hilton.

Oblivious to everything but the task at hand, Baxter did not note the time until it was too late for him to make the basketball game. But he felt just as well satisfied. He had completed a fine day's work and now he'd go to bed and fit the information he had gleaned into the plan that rapidly was taking shape in his mind.

Baxter was reviewing some of the things he'd have to memorize. The guy had been a three-letter man in Valley Falls High School and in college. Been a halfback in football, a high-scoring forward in basketball, and a catcher in baseball. A big-league prospect. . . .

Oh, yes, he mustn't forget that Hilton had been given the trophy basketball by his teammates the very first

21

time Valley Falls had won the state championship. Both papers had printed a photograph of the serious-eyed athlete, so uncannily like his son, holding the championship ball.

After a time he dropped off to sleep, his mind at ease now that he had roughed out his plan in which J. P. Ohlsen now definitely was cast in the role of the Valley Falls fall guy in his newest "get-rich-quick" project.

It was just as well that the stranger did not try to make the Valley Falls–Delford game. He wouldn't have had a chance. Ohlsen Gym was packed by six o'clock. In fact, there was such a mob on hand that some of the season ticket holders found it impossible to get to their seats and had to stand throughout the game. This was a grudge game.

The noisy crowd was talking it up even before the Junior Varsity teams took the floor.

"S'pose Jinx and Rock will tangle tonight?" someone asked excitedly.

"Wouldn't be surprised!"

"Remember two years ago? Remember when Jenkins hit our manager?"

"Aw, he didn't hit him, he pushed him!"

"Well, pushed, then— What was that kid's name?"

"Greg Lewis, wasn't it?"

"Yeah, that's right! That's why Rock clocked him!"

"Rock did all right the last time they tied into one another!"

"Well, I got me a ringside for this one!"

"Think Browning can hold that big Henry kid? I don't!"

"So what? Think Delford can hold Chip Hilton?"

But little by little the shouting and the loud talking dwindled away as the crowd slowly crowded into the lobby and on into the gym and the reserved seats and the bleachers and then into the aisles and finally to the very floor itself where they squatted just outside the side and end lines of the court.

For the first time in their young lives, the Valley Falls JV's played to a capacity house. The JV games usually began at six thirty and only a few persons, parents and personal friends, would be on hand to cheer the Little Reds on to victory. But not so this night. Every inch of spectator-space in Ohlsen Gym was occupied. And the JV's responded nobly, playing as though they were the feature attraction. Fred Peck and Connie DeWitt were particularly outstanding, and Chet Stewart, assistant coach to Henry Rockwell, watched in amazement as his protégés completely submerged the Delford understudies by a score of 42 to 26.

While the JV game was in progress, the Big Reds were readying themselves for the coming battle. Chip, all suited-up, was sitting quietly in front of his locker, conserving all his strength, and thinking of the approaching game. Delford's big Red Henry was averaging thirty points a game and that meant trouble. Then there was Jenkins, the Delford coach. A tricky character and a poor sport. Why would a self-respecting Board of Education keep on a man as cordially hated by every team that played Delford?

Worst of all, Delford's players took after Jenkins. They played rough and dirty . . . used a lot of dirty little tricks when the officials weren't looking, like pulling a fellow's belt, and tripping, and even punching you in the ribs if you turned your back. Rock was wise to that, though, and always warned the fellows that Jenkins used that method to get a fellow to lose his head and start a fight and get thrown out of the game. Rock said that winning from a fellow or a team like that was the best way to even up the score. . . .

Chip heard a burst of cheers from the gym and he knew that Delford was on the floor. A moment later he found himself out on the court dribbling the ball toward the south basket. The outburst of frenzied cheering from the Big Reds fans drowned out Delford's rooters and his thoughts and just about everything else.

"YEAAAAA VALLEY— YEAAAAA FALLS— FIGHT! TEAM! FIGHT!"

Chip's teammates followed him in that dash toward the south basket, and while Dink Davis led the cheering squad and the fans through a series of cheers, Chip and his teammates went through Rockwell's pre-game warm-up drill with dash and pep. They had this drill down pat and their fast passes and expert shooting brought roars of appreciation from the fans.

On the other side of the court, "Jinx" Jenkins, his face sullen and flushed, as usual, was following every movement of Chip and his teammates. Jenkins stood in front of the visitors' bench with his feet spread wide apart and his hands on his hips. His very posture indicated his belligerent nature.

The referee's whistle summoned Chip to the center circle where Red Henry joined him. Chip was a good six foot two, but he had to look up to meet the Delford captain's eyes. They matched hard grips and eyed one another steadily as the referee ran through the usual pre-game talk.

"Captain does the talking for the team. Game's the usual four eight-minute quarters. Ball's in play at all times unless it hits the basket supports or the back of the board. Watch the three-foot lines for the out-of-bounds passes! We're going to call it if you crowd the man out of bounds. Guess that's it. Let's have a clean game!"

Chip extended his hand again, but Henry ignored it

and turned abruptly away to join his teammates and Jenkins at the side of the court. Rockwell was waiting for Chip. After a brief word and a silent grip of six right hands they all joined in a "Let's go!"

Red Henry got the tap and it was Delford's ball. The visitors formed their attack leisurely and Chip matched his opponent's steps with a long, drag slide which kept his feet in position for a quick start. Henry had moved to a position on the free-throw line and Taps Browning was playing him cautiously, keeping a short distance away so he could switch if Delford attempted a pick-off on Henry or tried to "split the post."

But Delford wasn't trying any fast-moving plays. As a matter of fact, it was just the opposite. They passed and cut, passed and cut, using a roll attack which carried the four players moving the ball from one corner to the other and then back again. Chip and Speed and Red and Buzz kept walking and sliding with each roll, expecting their opponents to drive suddenly through or over and around and in to the basket. But nothing happened and it dawned on Chip that nothing was going to happen. Delford was going to slow down the game, hold the ball, use a "freeze" attack.

Chip thought that over a second and started to call for a time-out, but realized that he couldn't call "Time" until Delford had scored or the Big Reds got the ball. From the Delford bench Jenkins' bellow of "move, move, move" became monotonous, and the Big Reds continued to slide while Delford continued to pass and cut, pass and cut, and pass and cut.

When the crowd realized the situation and understood the strategy Jenkins was using, the cheering changed to one continuous roar. And that's the way it went until the crowd picked up the count somewhere and began to chant every time Delford passed the ball.

"Fourteen, fifteen, sixteen, seventeen, eighteen, nineteen, twenty, twenty-one!"

There was a sudden lull on the count of twenty-one because Henry suddenly drove in to the basket catching Taps Browning unawares and took a pass to score the first basket of the game. Chip called "Time!"

The stands were buzzing now, and in the huddle Chip was buzzing too. "Look, gang, they're freezing the ball, using a delayed attack, and that means they won't take a bad shot. Look, we can play 'em a little loose and sag whenever we're away from the ball and try to gum up the middle. Okay? Another thing! On the offense we'll work for good shots, too. Close ones, sure ones! Okay? Let's go!"

The continuous roar from the stands had made it tough on Stan Gomez, WTKO's local announcer, while Delford had been employing its stalling game. Now the time-out lull gave him a chance to explain to his listening audience just what was happening. And it gave Mrs. Hilton and George Browning and Mrs. Browning a chance to hear something over the radio in the Hilton living room besides the bellowing of a crowd of hoop crazy fans.

"Yes—it's a tough place to work a game—and I know you didn't get much of that first minute of play. As I said before, this is a tough place to work a game—here on the table—with the cheers and boos and yelling practically busting this mike to pieces. But it can't be helped and I'm hoping you'll stand by—stay with us.

"The count—the crowd-count you heard—that was the crowd counting the number of times Delford passed the ball—passed the ball before they took a shot.

"Yes, sir—they passed it twenty-one times—twenty-one times before they took a shot. And Delford now leads two to nothing. And fans—fans, that passing and the shot which ended it consumed exactly—exactly one minute and five seconds.

"Valley Falls called that time-out. It'll be their ball out of bounds at the north end of the court. Time's up—there's the referee's whistle—the ball's in play—guess I'll have to start yelling again.

"Morris passed the ball in—to Schwartz—to Todd dribbling down the right side of the court—in to Hilton now—he passes out—passes out from the keyhole—Morris has it—over to Schwartz on the far side of the court—back in to Browning on the free-throw line—out to Morris right here in front of us—Morris hooks it in to Hilton on the lane—and Hilton *scores!*" The announcer's voice rose to a shriek.

Then the roar which had preceded the time-out and which had slowly gained in volume suddenly overwhelmed Stan Gomez's mike and Mary Hilton snapped off the dial and glanced at her wrist watch. She'd tune in again in exactly fifteen minutes. She'd heard Chip say hundreds of times that ball games weren't won in the first or the second or the third quarters but in the last quarter.

It was all over when Mrs. Hilton switched back to the game. The announcer's hoarse voice came over the air against a background of steady cheering.

"And so there it is fans—forty-one to thirty-four.

"But don't be fooled by that score. It was a tense game all the way—and there was more basketball packed into this one game than there was in last year's entire tournament at University.

"The first half ended—as you know—ended in a ten-to-ten tie score. And then in the third period Coach Jenkins of Delford changed his slow-moving offense to a pressing attack—a pressing attack which carried Delford to a thirty-three to twenty-one lead at the end of the third quarter. But Coach Henry Rockwell—the Rock to you—had one up his sleeve too—

"Yep—he sent the Big Reds back into that final stanza fighting mad—and the biggest Red of them all—basketball-wise that is—Chip Hilton—went point crazy and scored—get this now—scored exactly twenty points.

"Yes—I know—I know exactly what you're thinking. Impossible!

"But you're dead wrong—it's in the record—twenty points in eight minutes.

"Too bad Hilton didn't start his scoring a little earlier —he might have broken the Big Red scoring record of thirty-nine points.

"And say, friends, know who holds that record—that all time Big Red scoring record for a single game—a thirty-two minute game?—

"You don't? Well, you ought to know—the name was the same—Yep—Hilton—Yep—Chip's father.

"Bill Hilton—Big Chip to some of you—scored thirty-nine points in a game against Dane just twenty-five years ago.

"So—the final score—Valley Falls forty-one, Delford thirty-four.

"Pete's got the totals now and I'll give you the run down of the sco—"

Mrs. Hilton didn't realize she had snapped off that radio. She didn't know how to be rude to anyone. In fact, Mrs. Hilton didn't even know George and Mrs. Browning were in that room. . . .

Mary Hilton stood there with hands resting lightly on the radio, a wistful smile on her lips, thinking back through the years, and wholly unconscious of everything except a heartbreaking happiness which clouded her lovely gray eyes with tears of joy. "My son," she whispered. "Oh, my son—"

CHAPTER 4

HOME TOWN HERO

MRS. HILTON peered over Chip's shoulder at the story of the Delford game on the sports page of the *Post*. Chip stirred restlessly. "Aw, Mother, I wish you wouldn't believe everything you see in the papers!"

"But it says right there that you were the star and the difference in the two teams and it's written by Pete Williams! And Pete Williams is the best sports writer in town. You said so yourself!"

"Why shouldn't I? After stories like that—"

"Joe Kennedy says the same thing in the *Times*! They both can't be wrong!"

Mrs. Hilton gently pulled the paper out of Chip's reluctant hands and sat down in her easy chair to enjoy thoroughly what Pete Williams had to say about the game and about her son.

BIG REDS SHELLAC DELFORD
IN "BATTLE OF WITS"
SEESAW GAME WON IN LAST QUARTER
Hilton Scores 26

Valley Falls' state champions defeated Delford last night in a record last-quarter scoring spree to win by a score of

41 to 34. William "Chip" Hilton was the difference in the two teams as they battled on even terms through the first half to a 10-to-10 score.

Delford's first-half tactics of holding the ball on the offense were unexpected and Valley Falls fans were in a near-frenzy when the locals seemed unable to match the strategy. Delford has been one of the high scoring teams of the state to date this season, and local fans were all keyed up for a rapid-fire barrage of baskets. They got them, but not until the final quarter!

Delford set the pace of the first half when big Red Henry got the tap and then joined his teammates in passing the ball exactly twenty-one times before a shot was attempted at the basket which resulted in the first score of the game.

Coach Jenkins changed his tactics in the third quarter, his charges forcing the play by pressing the Big Reds all over the court. When the fireworks were over, Delford led, 33 to 21, and it looked as though the state champions were going to receive their first defeat of the season.

The final quarter was the wildest ever seen at Ohlsen Gym. The Big Reds, sparked by Hilton, suddenly caught fire and swarmed all over the visitors, intercepting passes, forcing held-ball situations and using Delford's own third-quarter tactics to dominate the play and pull up even in the score. Hilton, shooting with uncanny skill, racked in six straight goals in four minutes to bring the score to 33 all. Delford called time and Jenkins instructed his charges to resume their first-half strategy of holding the ball.

Rockwell countered this by calling time himself, and when the Big Reds came out of the huddle, it was to continue their forcing style to swarm all over Delford. Before you could say scat, Chip Hilton had stolen the ball to score and put Valley Falls in the lead for the first time. Thereafter, it was all Hilton. He scored on a set shot from the free-throw line, again on a follow-up, pivoted around when his opponent passed the ball in from out of bounds and intercepted the ball to score again. Hilton's last four points were made in exactly seven seconds and that brought the Big Red total to 41 and Hilton's personal point total to 26. The final score was: Valley Falls 41, Delford 34. Delford scored exactly one point in the final quarter while Hilton scored all of the Big Reds' points, exactly 20, to set a new state record.

Hilton has now scored a total of 146 points in six games for an average of slightly over 24 points per game. The play of the popular Falls captain is encouraging to all local fans, since his presence in the Big Red line-up is certain insurance that Valley Falls will retain its section leadership and have a good chance to retain the state title. Hilton, as every basketball fan in town knows, did not play last year due to a leg injury. But his exploits on the diamond last spring and on the gridiron this past fall testify to the wizardry of Doc Jones. Doc says the leg is stronger than ever and with two good legs and the hands and the shooting eye Chip possesses, all existing sectional and state scoring records are likely to be shattered.

The box score:

Valley Falls	G	F	PF	T	Delford	G	F	PF	T
Hilton, f	11	4	1	26	Lando, f	3	1	3	7
Morris, f	2	2	2	6	Helms, f	1	0	2	2
Browning, c	0	1	4	1	Henry, c	5	7	1	17
Todd, g	1	0	4	2	Tatum, g	1	1	4	3
Schwartz, g	1	1	1	3	McBride, g	0	2	1	2
Smith, g	1	0	0	2	Cole, g	1	0	0	2
Peters, f	0	1	1	1	Parry, f	0	1	2	1
English, c	0	0	3	0					
Totals	16	9	16	41		11	12	13	34

While Mary Hilton was reading about the Delford game, Chip was reading the front-page story of the pottery convention and exhibit. The story gave the history of the local pottery and J. P. Ohlsen's contribution to the industry and to Valley Falls. Chip finished the article and his thoughts jumped from pottery and from basketball to figuring how much money he now had in his college fund. Then he got to thinking about the mortgage which still remained on the big house. He knew his father had loved this big, old house and he knew his mother loved it just as much. She had told him many times how his father had been battling the mortgage and the expensive illness of his only brother at the time he had lost his life at the pottery. And Chip knew his mother had found it necessary to take a position in the Valley Falls telephone office and that at first her modest income had barely been sufficient to meet the little family's expenses.

Chip knew, too, that Valley Falls was blessed with a home town bank controlled by local interests and that the members of the board weren't the kind to make things difficult for a nice person like Mary Carson Hilton. And they had kept extending the loan until, finally, Mary Hilton had been promoted to day-supervisor at the telephone office and little Chip had lengthened out and dropped the "little" part of his name, and had got a job. Then the payments on the mortgage had been resumed.

The remaining mortgage on the house was still considerable, but Chip and his mother could see daylight now. As he sat there, Chip was trying to figure out some way he could turn the college fund over to his mother to apply on the mortgage and use some other means to defray his college expenses. Every time he had brought that up before, his mother had been hurt and had said that his college education meant more to her than twenty houses, and so that was that.

Chip was in a sober mood now, and when he got that way at home, he liked to go down in the basement and work in his father's lab. So he excused himself and made his way down the basement steps and unlocked the lab door and sat down to think some more about his future hopes and plans. Chip had wanted to follow in his father's footsteps and study chemistry and someday, maybe, be J. P. Ohlsen's chief chemist at the pottery. But sports meant so much to him that he had dreamed, too, of one day being a coach or a sports writer.

His mother's quick footsteps on the floor brought young Hilton's thoughts back to the present, and he began examining the pieces of ware he had decided to keep. Mr. Browning, the next-door neighbor, was in charge of the mixing department at the pottery, and he had assured Chip that these pieces were superbly molded and of excellent quality. Chip's jaw squared as he looked at them. One thing was sure, college or no college, mortgage or no mortgage, he'd never sell them. He replaced them on top of the shelf and then began to browse through the typewritten formulas which were filed so carefully in the top drawer of the cabinet.

The tall stranger in his hotel room was up early that Sunday morning, too. He had decided upon a plan of action which he hoped would enable him to get at the formulas and ware that he now knew to be in the Hilton home. The kid was the answer to that problem. He had to get to know that kid well and use him as a key to the Hilton home. Well, the kid was all wrapped up in basketball and he certainly was well qualified to talk basketball.

So it was not strange that the newcomer to Valley Falls found his way to the Sugar Bowl that Sunday afternoon. But he was disappointed to find only Petey Jackson and his little brother, Paddy, in the store. In a way that turned out to be a lucky strike, for if there was one person in the world who was completely hoop crazy, it was Petey Jackson. A few cautious remarks and

Petey and his customer were on common ground.

"This seems to be quite a basketball town," the tall stranger said guardedly.

"Seems to be," Petey echoed, "*seems* to be!"

"Yes, what do you mean *seems* to be?" Paddy seconded aggressively.

"Why, just judging from the enthusiasm and the big write-ups the games get in the papers. But that's all right with me—I played the game a lot myself!"

Paddy's antagonistic attitude changed instantly. "You play now?" he asked, his blue eyes opening a little wider.

"No, I just fool around now, but I'm a pretty good shot!"

Paddy accepted that challenge immediately. "Bet you can't shoot as good as Chip," he said truculently.

The stranger lifted an eyebrow condescendingly. "Never heard of him," he said flatly.

That was too much for Paddy. "I never heard of you, either," he said truculently, rubbing a shock of red hair out of his eyes. "What's your name?"

The stranger smiled amusedly. "Baxter," he said softly. "T. A. K. Baxter."

Petey shook his head and eyed the stranger appraisingly. "You know something," he said slowly, "Chip Hilton's the best shot I ever saw and he's All-State. If you never heard of him, I don't think you know anything about basketball at all."

Paddy was shaking his head unbelievingly, "Never heard of Chip," he muttered. Then he turned to the stranger, again on the attack. "Where'd you play basketball?" he demanded.

"For the university," Baxter said nonchalantly, "up at State!"

"At State!" Petey sputtered. "Why you must have

been there about the same time Chip's father played. Did you know him? Big Chip Hilton?"

The stranger looked at Petey with surprised eyes and with his lips slightly parted. After a short pause he shook his head reluctantly. "No," he said, shaking his head again, "it can't be. Too much of a coincidence. The Bill Hilton I knew . . ." Suddenly he jumped up from his stool. "Say, come to think of it, though, he was from down in this part of the state somewhere. I wonder—"

Petey wasn't wondering. He knew. "Look, Mr. Baxter," he said confidently, "there was only one Big Chip Hilton that ever played at State! And that was our Chip Hilton's dad."

The stranger seemed completely nonplused. "I can't believe it," he said slowly. "It just can't be!"

Baxter definitely appeared to be greatly moved. He walked slowly to one of the tables in front of the fountain and dropped heavily to a chair. "Let me see," he said reflectively, "sixteen, seventeen, that would make it about twenty years ago." He slapped the top of the table. "You'd better bring me a coke after that. It could be, it could be—I'd sure like to meet that kid."

"That's easy," Petey said eagerly, "you just get down here any time tomorrow evening. Chip comes to work right after practice. Usually gets here about seven o'clock and works until eleven. He does the cleaning and the rough work in the storeroom. Say, what do you think about the zone defense?"

The stranger seemed to know all about the zone defense and all the other defenses, too. He digressed for the next hour on basketball. When he ended his discourse, Petey and Paddy had been completely captivated by the glib Mr. Baxter.

T. A. K. Baxter chuckled to himself as he made his way out of the Sugar Bowl. He had consumed three sandwiches, two plates of ice cream, four cups of coffee, and a coke. He and Petey had both been so engrossed in the basketball discussion that neither seemed to notice that Baxter forgot to pay his check.

After he left, Petey and Paddy talked of nothing else. "He's some guy, Paddy," Petey said enthusiastically.

Paddy nodded approvingly but his brow was furrowed. "What'd he say he was doin'?" he asked.

"Writin' a book about pottery. He's a big shot, Paddy! A real big shot! Chip'll sure be surprised about this."

Mr. T. A. K. Baxter appeared to be greatly pleased with himself as he walked back to his hotel. He always knew when he was on the beam and he enjoyed presenting a good performance. This afternoon he had been at his best. Of course, he chuckled, it was literally taking candy from a baby as well as sodas, sandwiches, ice cream, and coffee. He'd get around there often.

Some time later, Chip arrived at the Sugar Bowl and was mobbed by the brother act. Chip had never thought of Petey as an observant person, but he was agreeably surprised over how much Petey, supported by an eager Paddy, knew about the distinguished pottery authority, Mr. T. A. K. Baxter.

"Mr. Baxter played at State, Chip! *He knew your father!* He was a senior when your father was a freshman, but he played a lot of exhibition and pickup basketball with him. Gee, he knows more about him than I do, and I guess I knew your dad! And, Chip, he's writing a book about cer, cer— Yeah, that's right, ceramics, and he'd like to meet you and he said he'd drop in tomorrow night! He's a great guy! You'll like him, Chip. He's regular for such a big wheel!"

Paddy was a junior Petey in more ways than one. Petey had shut him out so far, but when that worthy stopped for breath, Paddy opened up.

"He's a great shot, Chip! Not as good as you, I bet, but he's good, and he shoots 'em all one-hand."

Petey had regained his breath. "Yeah," he interrupted, "he says you should shoot one-handed from any place on the floor. Says it's a faster shot and just as accurate even from a long ways out. He says a one-hand set shot is just like a two-hand set shot. You just get set and throw it the same way, 'cept you use one hand. Says you use one hand for close to the basket shots and that there's no reason you shouldn't use one hand for the long ones. He shoots his fouls with one hand, too."

Petey stopped again to catch his breath and Paddy rushed in.

"And, Chip, I bet he could be a great coach, 'cause he knows all about defenses and practicin' and scoutin' and, well, coachin'!"

Petey started pitching again. "Yeah, Chip, he knows all about freak defenses, such as three men out in front using man-to-man defense and two men next to the basket guardin' zone style, and well, more'n I ever heard about—"

Chip never said a word. He just stood there and listened to Petey and Paddy talk about a man who had really played on the same team with his father. Of course, Mr. Schroeder, Doc Jones, Rock, and lots of other persons had known his father and had seen him play, but that was different from playing on the same team with someone. Even coaching a person was a lot different than playing with a fellow who knew how you felt about things. Of course Rock had been his father's coach, just as Rock was his coach, and Rock was a lot like a teammate, even though he was a pretty tough guy when it came to discipline and hard work, but it was a little different. He'd sure be available tomorrow night.

CHAPTER 5

DEADEYE DICK

VALLEY FALLS HIGH SCHOOL was basketball crazy, and any fellow who was lucky enough to make the varsity squad was envied by every boy, and adored by every girl, in school. Chip thought all the fuss about basketball players was nonsense and spent as little time as possible in the halls where the heroes held forth for the benefit of charmed circles of basketball addicts. Instead, he usually lit out for the gym or the athletic offices when he had a free period and could get excused. Today, he was just a bit disappointed in his English teacher, Miss Barker.

In the test which he had just completed, she had asked for a five-hundred-word theme on the subject, "Why Basketball Is an Important Extracurricular Activity!" What was getting into Miss Barker, anyway? Was she getting like everyone else in Valley Falls, hoop crazy? Usually, she was interested chiefly in whose contribution was most important to the *Sir Roger de Coverley Papers*—Addison's or Steele's? Or she would hit everyone in the class with an assignment such as, "summarize the reason in Burke's *Conciliation of the*

38

American Colonies for the fostering of the fierce spirit of liberty in the New World."

He handed in his paper and struck out for the gym. In the gym office, which was across the hall from that of Prof Rogers, the director of physical education and athletics, Chip met Chet Stewart. The balding, assistant coach grabbed Chip by the arm, relief in his face.

"The answer to my prayer! Look, Chip, hurry into the gym and take my class. Prof Rogers wants me in his office right away."

"But what'll I give 'em? What'll I do?"

"Nothing! Just keep 'em busy until I get back! Teach 'em some basketball."

Stewart hurried away and Chip walked through the gym office and on out onto the gym floor. There he was greeted by catcalls and gibes from the thirty or forty freshmen who were sitting on the floor and leaning back against the wall.

"Go away!"

"Yeah, way off!"

"Go play basketball!"

Chip laughed good-naturedly.

"That's just what we're going to do," he announced, "play basketball! We've got twenty-five minutes left and that's just enough time for two half-court games of ten minutes each. Now, I want the best eight players. You fellows know who they are. Come on, step forward."

Eight boys were shoved forward, and Chip recognized Fred Peck, Connie DeWitt, Skinny Newcomb, Bob Todd, and one or two others. Then he saw the colored boy standing at the end of the line. The boy was almost as tall as himself but extremely slender. He was still protesting to the three or four boys who had pushed him out of the crowd.

In a very few minutes the eight teams were organized

and the first games were under way. Chet Stewart, Rockwell's faithful assistant coach and disciple, had long ago struck on this way of giving a large class a good workout and keeping them interested. It wasn't a bad way to discover good prospects, either.

When the bell rang, Chip was thrilled by the cheer the class gave him, although he knew it was just a bit of horseplay every group engaged in when the period ended. But the feeling passed quickly and there were two tight, little frown lines between his eyes when he walked slowly from the gym and out into the hall.

Stewart came tearing out of the opposite door and they nearly collided. "Thanks, Chip," he gasped, "thanks a lot. How'd it go?"

"Fine, Chet. Er, say Chet, did you ever notice that boy Barnes, Clem Barnes?"

"You mean the tall, skinny, colored kid? Sure! Nice kid! Why?"

"Well, I just think he's going to be a great player, that's all."

"Hey, I never thought about that—that is—"

Chip hesitated a second and then plunged. "He's a lot better than Fred Peck and Connie DeWitt, Chet— right now!" He watched Stewart closely, his clear, gray eyes narrowed a bit and focused straight on Chet's thoughtful face.

A brief smile swept across Stewart's mouth and then he pursed his lips and nodded uncertainly. "Yes, Chip," he said thoughtfully, looking up into the sober eyes of the tall youngster, "I know he is. Maybe I can do something about that."

The tension was gone, then, and the smile these two friends exchanged was deep and true. Chip turned quickly and hurried away, but Chet Stewart stood there a long minute, looking down the deserted corridor, enjoying the full measure of that moment of complete understanding which all too seldom passes between coach and player. Then he turned abruptly about and headed down the hall for Rockwell's private office. He needed Rock's advice.

Coach Henry Rockwell had been at Valley Falls from the very beginning of his coaching career. He had seen practically every grown man in town come and go through high school and practically every one of those men respected and admired him. To Mrs. Rockwell, he was Henry, to his close friends and a few of his school associates, he was Hank, and to every athlete who had played for him and to every sports fan in town, he was "Rock."

That "Rock" was fitting, everyone agreed. But to which of his attributes it best applied was a matter of varied opinion. Some thought the name was apt because of his stubborn nature, many because of his adherence to certain iron-bound sports principles; countless athletes and others who had visited his office for help of one kind or another knew it was appropriate because of his strength of character. Chet Stewart was one of these.

Rockwell scarcely looked up from the papers he was grading when Stewart entered. He knew the ring of Chet's footsteps well, and he knew the man who was his chief assistant and most trusted friend inside and out.

"What is it, Chet?" he asked softly.

"Er, Rock, it's about Clem Barnes."

"Barnes? Clem Barnes?"

"I don't think you know him by name, Rock. He's a colored boy I have in one of my first-year classes. And he's a good basketball player!"

"That make you mad?"

"No, but it might make some of the kids on the JV squad mad!"

"Don't get it!"

"Well, you will! You'll get it if he starts in one of the JV games in the place of DeWitt, or Peck, or Connors, or Rice, or Hill."

Rockwell suddenly straightened up in his chair and carefully placed the paper he had been reading on top of a stack of similar papers. His black eyes were alive and intent now, his thin lips were pressed tightly together, and the deliberate manner in which he spoke indicated that he was deeply stirred.

"Chet, a coach builds up a lot of personal principles during a coaching career. Some of those we start out with develop weaknesses as we gain in experience, and some improve with age. High on the list of those principles which I have found strong and right through the years I've been coaching is one which fills the bill right here. Know what it is?"

Stewart shook his head uncertainly.

"The best player gets the job!"

Stewart started to speak, but Rockwell's raised hand checked him.

"I didn't finish, Chet," Rockwell said softly. "The best player gets the job irrespective of race, creed, or *color!*"

There was a long silence in that little office, the kind of silence during which the thoughts of two persons who have been long associated seem to meet and speak more distinctly and understandingly than spoken words permit. Then Stewart brushed his hand back over the thinning hair of his head.

"He's never come out for the team, Rock—" he began uncertainly.

Rockwell's smile was one of understanding. "I know what you mean, Chet. But isn't it your job and my job to get the best boys in this high school, any and all of the best players, *out* for the teams and isn't it our job to put the best players *on* the teams? We don't ask a boy what church he attends. And we haven't any right, as long as a boy is a regularly enrolled student in this school, to overlook him because he is brown, black, or white."

Stewart wheeled and left the room without another word, but the abruptness of his departure was not meant to be discourteous. It was just his haste to rectify a mistake he knew he should never have made. Rockwell knew just where Stewart was going and just what he was going to do, and the little sigh which followed the sound of Chet's hurrying footsteps was one of relief and content.

Long after Stewart had gone, Henry Rockwell sat in that little office and thought back through the years to all the problems which had come and gone; the big problems and the little ones and the problems which had seemed to be almost impossible to whip at the time but had faded away almost from memory with the passage of time. Then he glanced at the clock on the desk and he began to think about his present basketball team.

Rockwell knew basketball and he knew boys. He knew that he had one of the strongest teams he had ever coached. He knew, too, that the boys knew they were good. They were confident to the point of being cocksure. One of his coaching axioms was to drill a team hard after an easy victory and easy after a defeat. That afternoon he poured it on the Big Reds because they were well rested after the Sunday layoff and because they had won two victories in two days and he wanted them to realize that two wins or six wins did not make a successful season.

Chip was dead-tired at the end of practice. After a shower and change to his street clothes he started out for the Sugar Bowl. He had been looking forward eagerly to this evening and his meeting with T. A. K. Baxter. Now, he kept peering out of the storeroom from seven until nine o'clock, but the stranger did not appear. Then, from nowhere, Speed and Soapy breezed in, brimming over with additional news about the stranger.

"What a shot!" Speed said breathlessly. "All one-hand stuff, Chip, and he hits from anywhere!"

"He's a dead shot, Chip," Soapy added, "a Deadeye Dick!"

"I heard some guys talking about him as I was coming down the street, but I didn't believe it," Speed said excitedly. "But I believe it now! Saw it with my own eyes!"

Soapy was just as enthusiastic. "Me, too," he chimed. "Saw it with my own peepers! The guy just can't *miss!*"

"He's still over there, Chip," Speed said. "Why don't you slip over for a few minutes and see for yourself. I'm going back! Come on, Soapy!"

John Schroeder was back in the storeroom at his desk. He looked up at the boy he regarded almost as a son and said softly, "Of course you can go over to the Y for a few minutes, Chipper. What's up?"

Chip told his employer about the sharpshooting stranger and was not surprised shortly after he had reached the Y gym to see John Schroeder and Doc Jones come puffing onto the floor. Chip had slowed down when he reached the top of the steps leading to the gym and had slipped quietly to a seat in the bleachers on the side of the court.

Out on the floor, a tall man garbed in a white T-shirt and shorts was bouncing a basketball on the floor and talking to a group of fellows who played on the Independents, the town team. Chip judged the man to be about six feet three or four. He was well put together, all right, but he showed the effects of an easy life by the small paunch which he carried. His muscles had evidently once been long and lean and hard, but they were flabby now and Chip's opinion of the man dropped. T. A. K. Baxter might have been a player at one time but he surely couldn't be much now.

The stranger changed that opinion pronto. He moved up to the free-throw line and began shooting. Each shot was a one-hander and he never missed. He didn't spend much time on the shot, either. Rock made the boys take their time, and take a deep breath, and concentrate. This man simply fired the ball through the hoop as quickly as one of the fellows threw it back. Then he began to move farther away from the basket and around the court. Every shot went spinning fast and true through the ring as clean as a whistle. He was good! Maybe great was the word, Chip thought admiringly as he started for the steps. He turned for one last look and then glanced at his employer. John Schroeder hadn't moved. Neither had Doc Jones. These two basketball enthusiasts were completely absorbed in the expert marksmanship of the tall stranger.

Petey Jackson was waiting expectantly. "How is he?"

Chip nodded his head approvingly. "Everything Speed said he was, Petey. The best I ever saw! Gosh, he *never* misses!"

Petey was highly gratified. "What do you think of one-handers now?" he asked.

Chip shook his head thoughtfully. "I don't know, Petey, but I guess I'll go along with Rock on the real long ones. As the coach says, it seems to me that a fellow can do most things better with both hands than with one and I guess the same principle applies to the feet."

"What's the feet got to do with it?"

"A lot! When you've got your weight evenly divided on both feet you've got a steadier stance."

Petey reluctantly granted that point but countered with another. "How about the time element?"

Chip nodded. "You sure have something there, Petey. A fellow can get a one-hander away faster than a two-hander, but then again, on a long shot, you *have* time. Rock always says, 'If you have to hurry a long shot, don't take it!' "

Chip knew Petey and he could tell by his face that this discussion would last all night if he didn't move, so he made his way back to the quietness of the storeroom and tried to do a little studying. But thoughts of the stranger kept intruding, and finally, with a sigh, he put the books aside and leaning back in John Schroeder's chair began to debate the shooting question. In a way he was glad Soapy and Speed wouldn't be waiting for him tonight, for he knew that the "one-hand" argument would continue where Petey had left off. This was a weekday night and Rock expected his varsity players to be at home and in bed at eleven o'clock. Chip was excused because he had to work. He tried the books once again and found that, at last, he could concentrate.

John Schroeder and Doc Jones came in about ten thirty just as excited as Speed and Soapy had been.

"What an exhibition!" Schroeder said admiringly. "Why, Chip, I never saw anyone shoot like that in my life, and I've seen the Celtics and the Globe Trotters and the old Buffalo Germans and about all the great college shooters like Luisetti and Mikan and Lobello and, well, all of them."

"You'd have to see it to believe it," Doc Jones added. "He shoots as though he had a patent on shooting!"

Fortunately for Chip, Petey chose that moment to

stick his head in the door and gesture violently. "He's out front, Chip," he whispered excitedly. "Come on!"

For once in his life, Chip was glad to get away from his kindly employer and genial old Doc Jones and he quickly followed Petey out to meet the stranger.

T. A. K. Baxter had sized this boy up well and he was smart enough to put on an air of great modesty in discussing his skill with a basketball. He made light of his accuracy by saying, "Oh, anyone could learn to shoot like that if he's been at it as long as I have."

As they became better acquainted, Baxter seemingly let Chip be the one to lead him into a discussion of the Bill Hilton he had known at State. He professed to be doubtful at first but, as he skillfully pieced the events of the "twenty or more years ago" together, he appeared to become more and more convinced that Bill Hilton was in reality Big Chip Hilton and that this youngster was Bill's son.

"What a coincidence!" he finally remarked. "Who'd have believed it possible after all these years! I'll drop in tomorrow night and we'll chat some more. We've got a lot in common, son."

Baxter extended his hand and they exchanged firm grips. "Good night, son," Baxter said smilingly.

Chip was thrilled. Why, Mr. Baxter was a swell guy. It sure proved that you couldn't tell a person by the way he looked in a gym suit.

Chip's mother was waiting up for him when he arrived home. But that wasn't unusual. Mary Hilton never retired for the night until Chip was safely home. The short half hour they spent together before bedtime was their chief opportunity to discuss the events of the day. And the news tonight was precious to both. Ever since the evening before, Mary Hilton had looked forward to more news of the man who had been one of Big Chip

Hilton's college friends. Chip told his mother all about the great shooting skill of Baxter and of his conversation with the man at the Sugar Bowl.

"He's very nice, Mother, and he knows all about Dad."

Mary Hilton was pleased with the news and pleased with the impression T. A. K. Baxter had made on her son. She was already planning the dinner she would serve when the stranger accepted their invitation to visit with them some evening. It would be pleasant to listen to her husband's old friend talk of his college days with Big Chip.

"How long did he say he was going to be in Valley Falls, Chip?"

"Why, he said he expected to be here a month or so getting material for a new book he's writing."

Mary Hilton's eyes sparkled. "I'll tell you what, Chip! We'll ask him to come to dinner next Sunday afternoon —and you can ask Soapy and Speed and Biggie to come along."

"You forgot Taps."

They both laughed and both were still laughing when they said good night a few minutes later. Valley Falls' six-foot six-inch center got his mail next door and his father and mother lived there, but Taps spent more time at the Hiltons than he did at home.

There were tears in Mary Hilton's eyes as she kissed her son good night. The years had healed somewhat the poignancy of her grief over Big Chip's tragic death. And now, suddenly, the gates of memory had jarred open. Out of the past had come someone who had been Big Chip's friend—someone who could share with her precious memories of Big Chip in the days when he was away at school and when she was waiting for him to come back to her. If only she could make Mr. Baxter's coming mean as much to her son as it meant to her.

CHAPTER 6

ONE-HAND SHARPSHOOTERS

CHET STEWART knew and had time for only one kind of basketball—the kind taught by the man who had been his high school coach and who was now his boss, Henry Rockwell. Chet had heard about the great shooting of the newcomer down at the Y and was a bit disturbed by the effect the man's remarks and one-hand shooting skill was having on his JV team and some of the members of the varsity. So it was not strange that Stewart should be numbered among those present when he learned that T. A. K. Baxter had been coaxed to present one of his shooting exhibitions that night at the Y.

While Stewart sat in the bleachers at the Y that night watching Baxter talk to members of the Valley Falls Independents, a team made up of former high school and ex-college players, his thoughts turned to certain difficulties which had arisen within the past few days on his JV squad.

Baxter's influence upon Valley Falls' basketball wasn't all that Stewart had to worry about. He had asked Clem Barnes out for JV practice and had immediately run into trouble. Not that there was a rebellion of any kind

49

among the members of the squad, but he noticed a clumsy awareness in the actions of the starting five, Fred Peck, Connie DeWitt, Buddy Connors, Teddy Rice, and Ralph Hill. And Chet Stewart knew enough about most of those boys and their parents to realize that there were going to be some anxious minutes just as soon as Clem Barnes began to steal the limelight away from one of the JV regulars. What's more he knew that Clem was going to do that in the very first game in which he played.

The kids who made up the starting five on the JV team were representatives of families who might be termed Valley Falls' business and civic leaders. Teddy's father owned one of the hardware stores; Hillie's dad owned a clothing store; Connie's father was chief chemist at the pottery, and that was the way it went.

Clem Barnes' father washed windows and a number of his customers were the fathers of the JV regulars. Stewart groaned and almost wished he had taken that job in the bank back some few years ago when it had been offered to him. But the appearance of the tall stranger on the floor made Stewart forget all about Clem Barnes and his JV basketball problems.

Stewart had seen a lot of people shoot a basketball, but he had never seen anything like this and neither had the fifty or sixty other basketball fans who were seated in the Y bleachers. After watching Baxter for five minutes, Chet could understand why the guy could gain and hold the admiration of Valley Falls' hoop crazy kids and grownups. Baxter was hot! He hit from the corners, from the sides, and from deep down the middle. And every one was a one-hander. Chet whistled softly to himself and when he left the Y and walked slowly home his mind was filled with comparisons of the one- and the two-hand shot.

Friday afternoon at four o'clock sharp, a big red-and-white bus pulled away from the steps in front of Valley Falls High School loaded to capacity with the state basketball champions and their current season's hoop hopes. There were Prof Rogers, Coach Rockwell, Chet Stewart, Biggie Cohen, and the eight-man varsity consisting of Chip Hilton, Speed Morris, Soapy Smith, Taps Browning, Buzz Todd, Red Schwartz, Bill English, and Lefty Peters, the smallest man on the squad. Most of this group had appropriated all the front seats in the bus.

In the rear seats, there were the two JV managers, and the JV reserves: Spike Davis, younger brother of Jerry Davis who was vice-president of Valley Falls' largest jewelry store and Rockwell's bitterest enemy; Ralph Knox; young Bob Blaine, the chemistry teacher's boy; and one of the eleven Ferris boys. This one looked like Fred, but all the Ferris boys were called "Stinky," so it didn't make much difference which one it was. Sitting side by side and talking in muffled tones were the JV starting five. This group was seated in the big rear seat which extended clear across the bus. Midway in the bus, in the seat next to the window, Clem Barnes was sitting beside Chip Hilton.

Everyone was talking and laughing and thinking about the game that night with Dane. And every once in a while, into the mind of every boy in that bus, with the exception of Biggie Cohen, Chip Hilton, and Clem Barnes, the quiet boy with the sensitive eyes and the slow-wide smile, came the thought of the one-hand shot.

Chet Stewart gave a thought to the shot once in a while, too, but he didn't let on to Rockwell. It was just as well, for later that night Coach Henry Rockwell was to get a firsthand view of the impression T. A. K. Baxter had made on certain JV basketball players by the name of Teddy Rice, Buddy Connors, Fred Peck, Ralph Hill, and Connie DeWitt. For the budding Big Red JV stars had lost no time in putting their one-hand shooting skill into practice. And as a result, at the end of the half, Dane's future greats were leading by a score of 16 to 7.

Rockwell saw only the first half of that game, but he watched it with an amazed expression on his face and there was a questioning look in his eyes when he studied Stewart to see what effect the wild shooting was making upon his chief assistant. At the half Rockwell repaired to the Big Reds' dressing room to help ready his varsity for the feature game. It was just as well that he left, for the Valley Falls JV's came completely apart at the seams in the second half and absorbed a real trouncing from the jubilant Danes, 42 to 23.

In spite of the disappointing score, there were two Valley Falls representatives who got a kick out of that second half. Chet Stewart sent Clem Barnes in for Ralph Hill midway in the third quarter and Clem proceeded to get five baskets and a free throw for a total of eleven points in exactly nine minutes.

Barnes got his points without help from his teammates. He couldn't buy a pass, but he was talented enough to use that tremendous leap of his to follow-in the Junior Big Reds' long one-hand shots and to tap in the rebounds for scores. On the defense, he held the Dane JV's big shooting gun scoreless. There was a determined slant to Chet Stewart's jaw when the game was over and when he passed the varsity coming out on the floor.

Rockwell caught the 42–23 score before the scoreboard was cleared, but he said nothing to Stewart when Chet rejoined him on the bench.

Dane was "up" for the Big Reds. It was the only shot they would have at the state champs this year and they meant to make it interesting. They did! Taps Browning got the tap and Chip came in high from his left forward position to take the ball. Red Schwartz had broken for the basket from his right forward position, but he was covered and Chip passed the ball back to Speed Morris. Morris was the Big Reds' backcourt sparkplug and usually started the plays by passing the ball ahead to Chip or Taps Browning and cutting around the post for a return pass.

But Speed surprised everyone, including and particularly Henry Rockwell, by attempting a long one-hander almost from the point where he had received the ball. Chip and Taps were caught by surprise and by the time they had wheeled to follow-in, the Danes had the ball and were swooping down court with their famed fast break for an easy score. Speed and Buzz Todd brought the ball up court and this time it was Buzz who let a long one-hand shot go from the right side line. The ball never even reached the basket and again the Danes broke down to their basket, clamping Speed Morris with a two-on-one play, and Dane led, 4 to 0.

Chip called "Time" and formed the huddle under the Dane basket. "Hey, what's the idea?" he muttered, looking anxiously at Speed and Buzz. "Come on, let's get together."

When play resumed it looked as though the Big Reds were going to get together, for Schwartz took Speed's pass from out of bounds under the Dane basket, dribbled fast to the front court, passed to Chip, and cut around the Big Reds' captain to receive a return pass and take a wide open lay-up for the basket and two points. But that was the last under-basket score for the

Big Reds in the first quarter. When they gathered in front of the bench and faced an irate Rockwell, they were trailing Dane, 20 to 12.

Rockwell's tirade, however, was of no avail, for now the one-hand shooting fever had gripped everyone on the squad except Taps Browning and Chip Hilton. Speed, Buzz, Red, and even Soapy Smith, when Rockwell sent him into the game to replace Buzz Todd, began trying one-handers from any spot on the floor. The half-time score was 33 to 17.

In the locker room Rockwell was furious and he gave them all an angry dressing down. It seemed to help when the second half began, but by the time the fourth period had rolled around the one-hand sharpshooters were at it again and with four minutes left to play the Big Reds were eight points down. Chip called another "Time" and Rockwell, in desperation, replaced Todd and Schwartz with Lefty Peters and Bill English and sent in orders for the team to attempt shots inside the fifteen-foot area only. That did the trick and five quick scores by Taps and Chip enabled the Big Reds to pull the game out of the fire, 47 to 46.

The bus ride back to Valley Falls wasn't the ride of a victorious team. Nor did things pick up when they stopped for an after-game meal halfway home. Rockwell had given them another tongue-lashing right after the game. And much as they resented the bawling-out, each one knew that everything he had said was true.

"What kind of exhibition was that? And where did you pick up that kind of shooting? And where was the team play? And what's happened to the *two-hand* set shot? That question is meant for you Todd, and you, Smith, and you, Schwartz—

"And where was the cutting and setting up of the plays you're supposed to be noted for, Morris? And what happened to your left hand? You never took a two-handed shot all night!

"And why didn't you try a few more hook shots, Browning? But wait. I take that back. You have to have the ball before you can shoot! And the only way you could have got that ball away from some of the members of this team tonight was by tackling them! Might have been a good idea at that! Why didn't you think of that, Hilton? You're s'posed to be—I said supposed to be—the captain of this team! But I didn't see any changes after your time-out huddles. Maybe I ought to start holding the time-out huddles right in front of the bench. I will if I have to! If the captain of the team can't follow orders when they're sent in with every substitution that's made—

"State champions! Huh! Who were you trying to imitate? The JV's? What an exhibition that was! But they've got some excuse! They don't know any better. But the state *champions* ought to know better! State champions! Huh!"

Chip was glad to get out of that bus and into the shelter of home. So was everyone else. A twenty-eight car train might have helped, but a twenty-eight passenger bus was too small. Much too small when Rock was on a rampage.

If you had been looking for a hundred basketball players the next afternoon, you could have found them without much trouble and without much loss of time. Everyone in town knew and had known all week that come Saturday afternoon T. A. K. Baxter was going to give another shooting exhibition at the Y. And that afternoon the reports came in to Petey and Chip that the stranger had taken over the coaching of the town team and had made the statement that he could teach anyone to be a good one-hand shot in two weeks.

Later that afternoon, Doc Jones and John Schroeder got into one of their heated arguments about basketball in the storeroom. John Schroeder was of the opinion that the long one-hand shot was pretty to watch but that it was a threat to team play. Doc Jones disagreed. And Chip was caught in the middle of the argument.

"I don't know much about long one-hand shots," Chip ventured when his opinion was requested. "But I do know that fellows don't like to play with someone who takes too many long shots, no matter what kind they are."

That was as far as Chip would go. His employer and Doc Jones were still arguing about the issue when he went home to supper.

T. A. K. Baxter knew all about the hours and the doings of the Sugar Bowl, now. He knew the rush periods and the slack ones and he made it a point to arrive when Petey Jackson was least busy. The day before he had explained to Petey that he was extremely forgetful about small details and that if he ever forgot to pay his check to note it down and he'd settle it all up in a week or two. But Petey was too thoughtful to worry a great man like Baxter with such petty details and reached down in his own pocket or into the "tips" glass to cancel out the stranger's checks.

That Saturday night Baxter arrived at the Sugar Bowl right after the nine-o'clock rush hour. Before he left, he had satisfied his appetite "for free" and had been assured of a Sunday dinner at the Hilton home.

Later, if you could have listened in on T. A. K. Baxter in his hotel room, you would have been amazed to hear him apparently talking to Chip Hilton and Mrs. Hilton in low tones, reviewing dates and incidents that had happened years before "when Bill Hilton and I were at State."

Baxter was a thorough man in a way. Whenever he planned a project it was well thought out and every detail was rehearsed again and again. So far, the Valley Falls pottery proposition was progressing very well indeed. Why, it seemed as though all he had to do was pull a string and the parts of his plan fell directly into place.

He had made the acquaintance of about everyone of consequence in town with the exception of J. P. Ohlsen. But that was the way he wanted it. He wasn't quite ready for that meeting. The sports writers had been easy to handle. Pete Williams of the *Post* and Joe Kennedy of the *Times* had welcomed T. A. K. Baxter's arrival in Valley Falls enthusiastically. Baxter's one-hand shot had given them a new basketball angle to play up and they gave it the best they had. They went along with his pottery interest because it was wise to remember that this was a pottery town first, last, and all the time. Baxter cleverly let Kennedy and Williams maneuver him into a discussion of his forthcoming book and he talked just reluctantly enough to encourage them to expand on the information he gave so grudgingly concerning his personal business.

So that night, when T. A. K. Baxter tucked his slowly shrinking little roll of bills into his sock and then under his pillow, he felt highly gratified with his progress. Tomorrow he'd get one foot inside the door of the Hilton home by way of the Sunday afternoon dinner, and from that time on, things would really start to move.

CHAPTER 7

STORM SIGNALS

MRS. HILTON, Mrs. Browning, and Taps were bustling about the kitchen and Chip made himself scarce and went into the living room to read the papers. He turned immediately to the sports page of the *Times* and read Joe Kennedy's "Times and Sports." Although Chip was one of Kennedy's most consistent readers, what he read this Sunday morning brought no pleasure to his face. Instead, there was a furrow on his forehead as he read the sports columnist's sports chatter.

TIMES AND SPORTS

By Joe Kennedy

The Dane game . . . What happened? . . . Should have been by twenty instead of one. . . . Credit for victory solely due to stretch play of Hilton and Browning . . . Hilton held to 14 points . . . maybe that's the reason.

And what about the JV team which is supposed to be crammed full of varsity talent?

The pottery convention and exhibit is over but Valley Falls' basketball fans are learning more basketball than pottery from T. A. K. Baxter, noted chemist, who has chosen Valley Falls as a working spot pending the completion of a forthcoming publication to be devoted to modern ceramics.

The one-hand–two-hand shooting controversy is raging all over town. John Schroeder and Doc Jones are . . . as usual . . . on opposite sides of the fence.

Clem Barnes, first colored boy to play on a Valley Falls high school team in any sport, got in the JV game at Dane . . . Scored a neat, eleven points in nine minutes . . . Mean anything to you, Rock?

Could it be that the Big Red team drive is suffering because of Chip Hilton's high scoring? This reporter thought certain members of the team passed him up regularly.

Stratford this coming Saturday . . . That's the last of the easy ones . . . Ten tough ones in a row after that . . . All willing and several of them capable of spilling the Big Reds' championship repeat hopes.

Valley Falls Independents play the Steeltown Crescents Christmas Day afternoon at four o'clock at the high school gym . . . Good game . . . Good cause . . . Hospital Fund . . . See you there.

Chip finished the column and then tossed the paper on the sofa and retired to the lab in the basement. He was still there when Speed, Soapy, Biggie, and Taps came clattering down the steps. Biggie and Taps were as much interested in the meal to come as in the personal appearance at the Hilton home of the noted stranger, T. A. K. Baxter. But that wasn't true of Speed and Soapy. Speed could scarcely wait for Baxter to appear, showing his excitement by restlessly squirming and talking about Christmas and the holidays and the game, while Soapy digressed nervously upon the "small change" write-ups Kennedy and Williams had printed about the Dane game.

And then the great man came swinging jauntily along and up onto the front porch. He already knew the boys, and proceeded to captivate Mrs. Hilton and Mrs. Browning almost with his first words. While the ladies were busy in the kitchen, Baxter entertained the boys with his old-time basketball experiences. They were cleverly told and he held the boys enthralled. Naturally, he was in the starring role in most of the games he described, but he was clever enough to leave most of that to the imagination of the boys. He didn't talk much about Bill Hilton because he wanted Mary Hilton to be in on that part of his visit.

Mary Hilton's dinner was, as usual, a success. Afterward, sitting in the living room with Mrs. Hilton and Mrs. Browning while the boys were cleaning up the kitchen and washing the dishes, Baxter really turned on the charm.

Yes, he liked Valley Falls very much. Naturally, his chief interest was pottery but he liked sports in general and basketball in particular because he had played the game so much in his college days. His book would keep him here for at least a month. Yes, living in a hotel was lonely, but small-town hotels were quiet and it wouldn't be too bad, he guessed—

Baxter cleverly guided the conversation to pottery and kept it there. He talked about Bill Hilton's study of ceramics at State and referred to a number of experiments they had worked out together. Then, just as if he had pulled another string, Mary Hilton asked him if he would like to see the small laboratory in the cellar. Baxter could scarcely conceal his eagerness, but he said, yes, he would be delighted, in a casual tone of voice.

Chip had never been too keen about anyone inspecting his father's laboratory and it was necessary for Mrs. Hilton to use her greatest diplomacy several times to cover up Chip's obvious annoyance while they were talking and puttering about the room. But Baxter noticed nothing out of the way, apparently, while his quick eyes swept around the room noting in one comprehending glance the gas-fired kiln, the mixer, the wheel, the sink, and the jars of finely ground feldspar and soapstone and quartz and kaolin and clays of every color. The locked filing cabinet in the corner drew his attention, but he made no reference to its contents.

Before they left, however, he brought up the subject of formulas and Mary Hilton fell forthwith into the trap.

"Oh, don't say formulas to me. There used to be hundreds of them scattered all over the house until I threatened to burn them up. Then Chip bought that old filing cabinet over there, and now they're all safely locked up *and* I can keep my house clean."

Chip was shuffling his feet uneasily and again Mrs. Hilton tried to ease the situation. "Don't mind Chip if he appears annoyed, Mr. Baxter. He never allows anyone down here and keeps the door locked as if it were Fort Knox. I don't even have a key."

Later, upstairs in the living room, Chip covertly watched the stranger talking to his mother. Why couldn't he like this man? His deportment was perfect, but something was wrong. There was something . . . something he could not explain even to himself.

Before he left, Baxter told Mrs. Hilton that he intended to list some of Bill Hilton's formulas in the book and give him the credit he deserved and had never received. That was the clincher. Mrs. Hilton was overcome. But she remembered to invite Baxter to Christmas dinner.

Baxter said it was an imposition, but he gracefully consented to come because he knew she was influenced by the Christmas spirit. Christmas was an empty period in his life because he had never married and his parents were no longer living. He was honored and grateful for the privilege of sharing the holiday in her home.

That night Chip couldn't get to sleep. His mother and he had, after a long discussion, agreed to ask Mr. Baxter to move to the Hilton home for the month he would be in Valley Falls. Chip hadn't been keen about it at all. He had tried several excuses. "It would be added work and a lot of trouble and only a little income and—"

But Mary Hilton had overcome all his objections. Mrs. Browning would take care of the gentleman's room and would make coffee for him every morning. The house *was* too large for just the two of them, and the few dollars *would* add a little to the college fund—

Chip wanted his mother to be happy above everything else. He wasn't home very much in the evenings and it would be nice to have someone in the house to keep her company until he got home.

Then the team and the Dane game occupied his thoughts and he forgot Baxter completely in his attempts to figure out the little changes which were taking place in the team. What had happened to Buzz Todd? Buzz was the best two-hand shot in the state and here he was taking long, crazy one-handers. And all the other fellows were trying them. That brought him back to the stranger and his one-hand shooting. Chip had a hunch that meant trouble and it was with that thought that at last he fell into a restless, uneasy sleep.

But T. A. K. Baxter had no trouble getting to sleep that night. He knew it had been a day of real progress. He had noted the quick expression of sympathetic understanding which swept over Mrs. Hilton's face when he said the hotel was a bit lonely and he had been invited back for Christmas dinner. He knew that on that day, just as if he pulled a string, she would ask him to move into the Hilton home for the duration of his stay in Valley Falls. He smiled to himself and sighed in satisfaction.

Everything would be just right then. Mary Hilton worked all day and the kid was at school and he'd be alone with plenty of time to get into that laboratory and into that filing cabinet and then he'd be ready for J. P. Ohlsen.

But he'd have to be careful about that kid. The kid didn't like the idea of anyone messing around in the lab. He'd have to play it smart. The kid was more than just a high school athlete. He was nobody's fool and his suspicions might easily be aroused.

CHAPTER 8

DRUGSTORE COACH

CHIP wanted to sleep late the next day. It was the first day of the ten-day Christmas vacation and there would be no school until Thursday, January 2. But habit was too strong and he was up, as usual, before his mother left for work. When he crossed the room to close the window he had a surprise. The first real snow had fallen in Valley Falls and the wish of many people for Christmas snow looked as though it was going to be fulfilled. Chip spent the hour after his mother left shoveling snow off the sidewalk and puttering around the house. Then, restless with the inactivity, he hurried down to the Sugar Bowl and repeated the performance.

As Chip worked, his thoughts shifted from one thing to another. First, he thought of Baxter, the man who knew so much about his father. Then he thought about the team and the crazy one-hand shooting which seemed to have become almost a disease with every basketball player in town. His thoughts shifted again. This time they turned to Clem Barnes and he felt good because Clem had made such a fine showing in the Dane-JV game.

Chip chuckled when he thought of the compliments Clem had received in Pete Williams' and Joe Kennedy's columns. That probably was the first time Clem Barnes ever had seen his name in the paper. But it wouldn't be the last time. Then Chip thought of the plans he and Clem had made to practice at the Y gym every morning. Ty Higgins, the gym director, always had let Chip practice at the Y gym when it wasn't in use and he had said, "Sure it's all right to bring Barnes," and so he and Clem had decided to practice every morning during the holidays at nine o'clock.

Chip was puffing a bit now as he tried to force his thoughts to keep pace with his shoveling and he stopped to rest and get his breath. But Clem Barnes was in his mind and he began to concentrate on the things he had planned to teach the eager boy. He'd have to work on Clem's defense most of all. Clem didn't know how to keep his weight back so he could move as quickly as his opponent. And Clem turned his head away from his man all the time. That was no good. Every good basketball player knew that the time to cut against a guard was when he turned his head. Clem would have to learn to use what Rock called peripheral or marginal vision, the kind of vision you use when you look straight ahead but sidewise at the same time. He leaned the shovel against his leg and stretched his arms out straight to his sides. Then he wiggled his fingers and, looking straight ahead, moved his arms farther and farther back until they were directly in line with his shoulders. Why, just as Rock said, a fellow could see them just as well looking straight ahead, if he concentrated.

During the holidays, Rockwell called regular practice at the usual time. There was no changing the Rock. Practice was practice and if you didn't want to practice, then you didn't want to play! However, on Tuesday, he grudgingly announced that the next practice would be held at the regular time Thursday.

And so Christmas came and Mrs. Hilton received a beautiful pin and bracelet from Chip and a big box of candy and a lovely poinsettia plant from T. A. K. Baxter. Chip got a lot of useful things to wear from his mother and a hand-tooled belt from Baxter. The Hilton holiday season was off to a happy start.

Chip and Clem Barnes practiced every morning at the Y and each boy learned much from the other.

Then suddenly Christmas was gone and T. A. K. Baxter moved to the Hilton home, on a generous business-like basis, of course. He was careful to let everyone know that it meant a great deal to him to dwell in the home where his friend Bill Hilton had once lived. And he turned on the charm for all the people he met and especially for Chip Hilton's pals.

The Valley Falls Independents played the Steeltown Crescents at the high school Christmas Day afternoon and won by a score of 93 to 81. It was the greatest number of points the Independents had ever made in a single game. In fact, it was the greatest number of points any Valley Falls team had ever scored and it made Coach Baxter. Everyone in town raved about the high scoring, the constant action, and the one-hand shooting of the locals.

"Why, every player on the starting five scored double figures!"

"Think of it! *Ninety-three* points!"

"And all *one-handers!*"

Only a few observers seemed cognizant of the fact that the Crescents had also scored a lot of points. But these few were real basketball fans who liked the game for its all-round play, balance between offense and defense, clever passing, the development and execution of sound plays and, above all, teamwork.

Practice the day before the Stratford game, Friday,

December 27, was the worst of the year. Chet Stewart's
JV's had practiced from one o'clock to three o'clock and
Chet came into Rockwell's office a short time later,
mumbling something about "Crazy basketball and
crazier half-wits who teach kids a lot of crazy darn
stuff!"

Rockwell usually got a kick out of Stewart's bulling,
but there was no humor in his eyes today. "Now what?"
he asked quietly.

Stewart slouched down in the chair opposite Rockwell's desk. "I," he said viciously, "have just been advised what's wrong with the kind of basketball we're
trying to teach!"

"That's interesting," Rockwell observed dryly. "Which
drugstore coach is it now? Jerry Davis or Doc Jones?"

"Oh, it's none of the local coaches. You've probably
heard of the *new* coaching genius in town? The great
Baxter? Well, today who shows up at practice? That's
right! The president of the National Federation for the
Development of the Long One-hand Shot in Basketball!
Yep, that's who it was!

"And he came to practice, if you please, at the invitation of Teddy Rice, Ralph Hill, and Spike Davis. Yep,
the Chamber of Commerce, the Lions Club, the Rotar-
ians, the Kiwanians, and some others enjoyed the presence of a guy named Baxter a couple of days ago at their
joint luncheon and he advised them that his chief hobby
in life was kids and basketball.

"Then he proved it by spending a morning with their
kids at the Y gym. And today he honored *me* with his
personal appearance at our practice."

"And?"

"And after he was properly introduced, of course, by
the youngest member of the one family in town which
gives you and me the most adverse advertising, the

Davis family, he proceeds to tell me that we're way behind the times in a few of our basketball principles—
That the two-hand set shot is no longer practical because and because and because and because—indefi-
nitely!"

Rockwell stirred in his chair and glanced at the clock
on the wall. "Time for practice," he said softly. "We'd
better get out on the floor before someone moves in and
takes charge. Let's go!"

Chip sensed something was in the wind the moment
Rockwell's whistle shrilled. He knew it the minute they
were seated in the bleachers and he saw the blackboard.
And when the Rock stopped tossing the piece of chalk
up in the air, Chip knew there was an important skull
session coming.

"Basketball is first, last, and all the time—a team
game! No team ever went far against good competition
just because it was composed of five great shooters, or
because it had five great guards, or five great passers.

"Last year this team won the state championship because it was composed of kids who played as a team.
There were no individual stars and no great scorers.
This year we have every one of those boys back with the
exception of two—Lennie and Howie Scott. And as a
substitute for those two, we have our captain, Chip Hilton.

"We're a good team! Maybe a great team! Maybe
we're good enough to repeat as section and as state
champions. But we're never going to do that playing the
way we've been playing and practicing during the past
two weeks. We barely scrambled through the Dane
game and we've looked pretty bad in practice ever since.

"Now I've been in basketball as a player and as a
coach a long time. I've seen good players and good
teams come and go. I'll probably see more. But I never

saw a team win a championship unless its players pulled together and played as a team.

"There's one more important item. Few great teams got that way without someone to lead and guide them. Someone has to take the responsibility for the coaching and the leadership. The coaching is my responsibility. You elected your own leader, Chip Hilton.

"As the coach, it's my job to get you in shape and keep you in shape, to outline a style of play offensively and defensively, to place the best players in the various jobs and to keep them there unless they prove detrimental to the team, to scout the opposition whenever possible, to use all the experience at my command to assist you to win games, to teach you to play hard and play to win, to show by my deportment and language that I can be a modest winner and a gracious loser.

"It's my job to maintain and teach discipline and team spirit and team play and I'm going to do it! Now, I am fully aware that every boy likes to see his name in the papers, likes to score, and likes to play an important part in his team's success. But I am also aware that it isn't possible for every player on a team to take the leading part in every game, for there aren't enough leading parts. Someone has to be the feeder, someone has to be the driver, someone has to set up the plays, someone has to be the leech on the defense, and someone has to get the most points.

"Now, the way you fellows have been playing it's clear that each and every one of you wants to make the points. *All* the points! And you want to make them the hard way. As far away from the basket as possible! And —with *one hand!*"

Rockwell stepped quickly to the blackboard and sketched the outline of half of a court. Then he drew three curved lines extending from each side line.

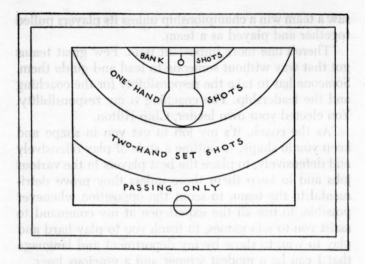

Tapping the blackboard to accentuate his words, he continued, "Under the basket, I expect you to swing your shoulders around on the shot and square them in a line with the basket before you release and bank the ball against the backboard.

"Between this bank-shot area and the line extending from the corners to the rear curve of the free-throw circle, I want one-hand shots. One-hand shots with the shoulders squared with the basket, just as they're squared in the bank-shot area.

"In the third area, in the *two-hand* set-shot area, you'll use only two-hand set shots. The first player who attempts a *one-hand* shot from this area will be benched! Is that clear?"

Rockwell paused and looked searchingly at each player. Then he continued in a milder voice, "Now, let's have a short workout and try to look like the team which won the state championship!"

The practice was short and terrible. There was no

drive, no pep, no desire to play. Rockwell sighed resignedly and sent them to the showers.

Not much was said by the crowd of boys in Speed
Morris' jalopy as the little car slid slowly along Main
Street, but when they reached the Sugar Bowl and were
sitting in the middle of the high school crowd at the
fountain, Soapy tried to be flippant. "Rock was in pretty
good form this afternoon, wasn't he?"

"We had it coming!" Chip said flatly.

"Maybe," Speed said thoughtfully, "maybe we did
and maybe we didn't! I can't understand why he's getting all up in the air about the one-hand shot. Heck, it
counts two points just like a two-hander."

In the debate which followed, Petey Jackson was an
interested listener. But only for a short time. Petey
wasn't the type to listen very long. "Seems to me the
Independents are doin' all right with one-handers," he
said aggressively. "Could be Rock is a little jealous of
any kind of basketball, 'cept what he teaches, you
know—"

Chip lowered himself slowly from the tall, fountain
stool. "Could be," he said quietly, "but I seem to remember a long two-hand shot which won the state championship for Valley Falls last year!" Then he turned
abruptly away and made his way back to the storeroom.

Chip and Clem Barnes practiced at the Y for an hour
the next morning. Chip was pleased with the progress
Barnes was making. The slender boy was as fast as a
cat on his feet and he was quick to learn. Once he had
been told about a certain pass or shot, it wasn't necessary to drum it at him again. He was a natural.

The Valley Falls Junior Varsity starting five was composed of boys who had played in the West Side grade
school as a team and intact as freshmen. Now they were
almost ready for varsity duty and they were looking for-

ward complacently to next year when the varsity would be losing Hilton, Morris, Schwartz, Todd, and Smith. Then it would be their turn. Of course, Taps Browning and Lefty Peters and Bill English would be back, but they were more or less varsity reserves now, with the exception of Browning, and Rockwell wasn't the kind of guy to break up an experienced team like they'd be.

So busy were Fred Peck, Connie DeWitt, Buddy Connors, Teddy Rice, and Ralph Hill, thinking about next year as they sat all dressed for the game on the bench in the dressing room that they never even caught Chet Stewart's first words. But when they heard "—and Barnes at right guard" their heads jerked up in shocked surprise.

Barnes at right guard! Why, that was Hillie's spot! Was Chet kidding? Barnes had only been on the squad a week! What was eating Stewart now? Barnes a regular? A Negro on the starting five? So that was it! Well, he'd soon find out that starting and staying in there was something else again!

When they turned to look at Ralph Hill they saw he was staring at Stewart with his mouth half open, as if he didn't believe his ears.

So Ralph Hill, a regular member of the starting JV five, sat on the bench when the Stratford JV—Valley Falls JV game began and he was still wondering if it was true. And a lot of Valley Falls basketball fans who liked to see the Little Reds start off the evening's bill sat there, too, hardly believing it was true.

Up in the stands, Ralph Hill, owner of the leading clothing store in town, half rose to his feet and then sat down mumbling something, and then he joined Mrs. Ralph Hill in looking from their son sitting on the bench, to the colored boy out on the floor, and then back to the bench to the set face of the JV basketball coach.

Several townfolks looked at Hillie's parents, sitting there tense and white, and there was a lot of whispering.

"A colored boy in Ralph Hill's place?"

"There's going to be a lot of trouble about this!"

"A Negro boy! What do they need him for?"

"I wouldn't want to be in Stewart's shoes when this game's over."

"Nor Rockwell's either. He's responsible! He's in charge!"

"That Negro boy better be good!"

They didn't have to worry about that part of it. Clem Barnes was the best player on the floor and scored eighteen points in the twenty-four-minute game. Still, there was a lot of headshaking and frowning on the part of many of the fans in the stands. The Little Reds won easily from the Stratfords and Ralph Hill got in for most of the game, but not in place of Clem Barnes.

Chet Stewart kept Barnes in the game for the full twenty-four minutes. One by one, the previous regulars replaced each other in the line-up, and as each change was made, another family became incensed because of Chet Stewart's unbelievable action of inserting a colored boy on a kid team which had played together for three years and which was composed of boys representing the "best" families in town.

The varsity game was anticlimactic. Everyone was talking about the colored boy, and the failure of the fans to cheer and lift the Big Reds out of their doldrums was nearly responsible for the first defeat of the season.

Stratford was supposed to be a push-over. But it was a tough game every second of the way. The Big Reds still showed the effects of the week of desultory practice. Buzz Todd, Speed Morris, Red Schwartz, and Soapy Smith were still sold on the one-hand shot and tried the shot every time they got a chance in Rockwell's one-hand shot area.

Chip had never felt more out of a game in his life. He and Taps received the ball from their teammates only when a shot was impossible and, consequently, the attack bogged down. But sheer personal ability enabled the Big Reds to stagger through to win by a hair, 44 to 40. Chip managed to get twelve points, making him the high scorer for the Big Reds.

At the start of the second half, Rockwell had benched Buzz Todd and Red Schwartz, replacing them with Lefty Peters and Soapy Smith. And a little later, when Soapy tried a one-hander just a little outside the one-hand shot area, Bill English came in to relieve him.

The crowd filing out of Ohlsen Gym wasn't the usual happy, cheering, laughing, and loud-talking crowd which departed after a Big Red victory. It was a low-murmuring, whispering crowd, puzzled and confused about a lot of things.

And the little band of basketball champions who piled into Speed Morris' jalopy were a quiet, thoughtful crowd, too. When Chip swung out of the car in front of the Sugar Bowl he was almost glad to get away from the tense atmosphere which had gripped his friends. Glad to get away and to get to work and to cleaning and closing up and glad to be walking home alone over the hard-packed snow even though it made the short walk a long one.

When he got home and found Baxter and Mr. and Mrs. Browning and his mother waiting, he was glad for the first time in a long while to hurry away to bed. Later, lying there in the dark Chip Hilton was a hurt, sad youngster and suddenly he almost hated T. A. K. Baxter for what he was doing to the team, to his friends, to the town. Baxter and his one-handers . . .

CHAPTER 9

THE STARTING FIVE

T. A. K. Baxter had a way with people and with locks. The lock on the laboratory door in the basement had been easy, but the lock on the filing cabinet containing Bill Hilton's formulas had stopped the sharpshooting locksmith cold. But not for long. After several unsuccessful attempts, he had solved that little problem by taking the number of the filing cabinet and writing directly to the company which had manufactured the file. He was careful to request that the key be mailed in care of the box he had rented at the post office.

The key had come through promptly and Baxter's plan was working out according to schedule. But there was a fly in the ointment. Mrs. Browning, anxious to take good care of her next-door neighbor's guest, came blundering into the house without warning at all times of the day. And that meant he had to time his visits to the laboratory just right. Then, too, he had to be extremely careful that everything was left just as he found it in the little cellar room.

Baxter had tried working downstairs in the laboratory but had decided that it was too dangerous. Now, each morning he brought the formulas to his room, one at a time, and replaced them each afternoon.

All in all, everything was progressing very well. He managed to get nearly all his meals "for free" between Mrs. Browning and Mary Hilton, and, of course, there was always the Sugar Bowl where he could maneuver a snack from Petey Jackson in exchange for a bit of basketball lore. Since he had assumed the coaching responsibilities of the Valley Falls Independents, and his one-hand fire department basketball clicked with Valley Falls' hoop fans, Petey Jackson had been completely in his power.

The Sunday sports pages carried a number of stories about the Stratford games and the progress the Valley Falls Independents were making. And in Joe Kennedy's column in the *Times* and in Pete Williams' story in the *Post* there were several references which reflected on the future of a new Junior Varsity star by the name of Clem Barnes.

Baxter was sitting in the Hilton living room early that Sunday morning reading Pete Kennedy's "Times and Sports" when Chip came down to breakfast. Baxter waved the paper as Chip came down the steps.

"Come here, Chip, look at this column of Kennedy's! Sorta got you fellows on the pan."

Chip reluctantly took the paper and sat down on the sofa. The first few lines were enough to put him on his guard and prepare him for Baxter's warning. That worthy's mouth was twisted in a little smirk of satisfaction as he fingered his small mustache and watched Chip's reaction to Joe Kennedy.

TIMES AND SPORTS
By Joe Kennedy

"FIFTY-FOUR FORTY or FIGHT" takes this reporter back to memories of school days and history . . . And last night's basketball game between Valley Falls and Stratford brings back memories of last year's state championship basketball team.

What has happened to the smooth play which carried last year's Big Reds from an underdog role to highest honors as the best team in the state? . . . How can a team . . . a veteran team . . . revise its form so completely?

Clem Barnes, the new basketball star on Valley Falls' sports horizon, stole all scoring honors for both games last night when he scored eighteen points in twenty-four minutes of play . . . Oh, yes . . . Chip Hilton was held to twelve points.

And Stratford nearly did what some Section Two rival is going to do any day now . . . Yep . . . the Big Reds are coming apart at the seams as surely as the Little Reds' Clem Barnes is one of the greatest basketball prospects ever to break into the basketball picture at Valley Falls as a freshman . . . Yes . . . that's right . . . a *freshman.*

Watching the play of some of Hank Rockwell's varsity stars last night brought a thought to this reporter's mind . . . Yes . . . that's right . . . Clem Barnes is playing better ball right now than two and possibly three members of Rock's state championship team.

Have you been watching the scores the Valley Falls Independents have been running up? . . . Rockwell's Big Reds could use a few more points . . . Can it be that Rock's antipathy to the long one-hand shots employed so effectively by the Independents is responsible for the sagging defense Big Reds' opponents always employ? . . . A long stab often opens up a sagging defense . . . Sure . . . everyone knows that Chip Hilton and Taps Browning . . . leading scorers of the Big Reds . . . score practically all their points within fifteen feet of the basket.

By the way . . . Clem Barnes has definitely shelved one of the Little Reds' veterans . . . And . . . from the mailbag this past week this writer received a number of bitter letters concerning the use of Barnes in the Dane game. . . . I wonder if any of you anonymous writers saw the game last

night? . . . Probably wouldn't mean anything to you, anyway . . . If you can't sign your name to a letter you probably can't add . . . So I'll do your schoolwork for you . . .
Barnes scored eleven points in nine minutes at Dane and
eighteen in twenty-four last night against Stratford and that
makes a total of 29 for 33 . . . nearly a point a minute.

Chip shook his head slowly as he finished reading the
column. That article meant more trouble. The little gap
which had appeared from nowhere in his friendship
with Speed and Soapy and Red and Buzz because of his
dislike for the long one-hand shot and because of his
interest in Clem Barnes would probably grow larger.

Chip was right about the tension which had crept
into his friendship with Speed, Red, Soapy, and Buzz
Todd. It was evidenced in the practices and at the Sugar
Bowl. It was an uncomfortable situation, but there was
no way to get at it without coming right out with a direct question. That seemed foolish in view of the fact
that there had been no open break of any kind.

Chip knew his friends resented his practices with
Clem Barnes at the Y gym each morning, but he wasn't
going to stop that. Not when Clem showed such a burning desire to become a good player.

So, before it seemed possible, Thursday, January 2,
and the first day of school following the vacation period
arrived and Chip was back in the routine of school,
practice, work, and study, and his mind was so busy
that he didn't have time to worry about the problem.

Coach Henry Rockwell was busy, too, but not too
busy to worry about several annoying matters. First on
the list was his team and the game with Dulane tomorrow night. Dulane was admittedly weak, had lost to
Clinton, the team Valley Falls had swamped a month
ago, but the Big Reds weren't the team they had been
at that time.

Rockwell had a hunch about the Dulane game. Maybe it was the way the practices had been going and maybe it was the little undercurrent of revolt which he had sensed in the boys. But he had a hunch that Dulane meant trouble. There were a couple of other matters which had upset Rockwell this morning. Here it was, the very first school day of the year, with New Year's resolutions little more than a day old, and certain extremely petty persons were writing him letters and calling him on the telephone about something which was none of their business.

Ever since the past football season, when there had been such a big to-do about one or two losses the football team had suffered, the animosity between himself and a few of the younger sports fans of the town concerning the coaching of the Big Reds had been acute. For the past two weeks, these fellows had aired their feelings with respect to Clem Barnes to such an extent that he had found it necessary to tell them in no uncertain terms to mind their own business.

But this morning some of the older and more stable citizens of Valley Falls had telephoned regarding Barnes. First, it had been George Connors who called and suggested lamely that Stewart use Barnes as a substitute rather than as a starter. "The kids have been playing so long together, Rock. It seems a shame to break up the team."

Then Jim Rice had called—big, boisterous, happy-go-lucky Jim Rice—wealthy owner of Valley Falls' big hardware store. "Hiya, Rock! Er, Happy New Year to you and the family! Say, what's this Teddy tells me about Chet Stewart throwing Ralph Hill off the JV's for a colored kid!"

And then, when another call came in from J. H. Davis, president of the Valley Falls Jewelry Company, the coincidence was too much. The whole thing was a put-up job, Rockwell decided, and the pressure just short of being antagonistic. But he held to his principles and explained his position much as he had explained it to Chet Stewart and suggested to each caller that the matter could probably be discussed more intelligently in a personal meeting. He assured each caller, too, that he would be glad to meet with him at any time and talk it over.

Rockwell sighed wearily and started on the pile of letters which had accumulated over the vacation. He came to a letter postmarked Tuesday, December 31. He read it slowly and thoughtfully, and when he had finished it, he leaned back in his chair suddenly tired and discouraged. The letter he had just read disturbed him more than all the telephone calls, one-hand shots, drugstore coaches, and the worries of coaching a state championship team put together. He looked at the signatures. Yes, they'd all signed it; all except Ralph Hill.

Just then the telephone rang again and Rockwell reluctantly picked up the instrument. This time it was Bob Blaine, head of the Valley Falls High School chemistry department and one of Rockwell's best friends. Blaine was known to every student and every person in town as "Prof." Rockwell, holding his breath, waited for Blaine to begin. Surely Prof wouldn't give him the same line he'd been listening to all morning.

"Hank, young Bob has told me something about the difficulties Stewart has been experiencing with the JV team and also something about a letter. Have you received it? Just reading it—? Well, Hank, I'd just like you to know that young Bob told me last night that he was a little ashamed of his part in that letter and, well, I guess you know how it is with kids and how they stick together no matter how they feel inside better than I do. And, Hank, if I can help in any way—"

Rockwell felt a little better when he said good-bye to Blaine, but when he turned back to the letter and read the scrawled words on the sheet of paper, his chin line slackened again and his eyes were deeply troubled.

Dear Coach Rockwell:

We know you know about Clem Barnes taking Hillie's place on the team and we hate to bother you, but we know you don't like to see a winning combination broken up and we'd like to ask you to ask Chet Stewart to put Hillie back on the starting five and use Clem as the sixth man. We like Clem all right, but we play better with Hillie.

Yours truly,

Fred Peck
Connie DeWitt
Buddy Connors
Teddy Rice
Spike Davis
Fred Ferris
Bob Knox
Bob Blaine

Coach Rockwell made up his mind to be on hand that afternoon at the Little Reds' practice session.

Nine of the ten boys who reported that afternoon for JV basketball practice were extremely nervous. The usual locker-room chatter and horseplay was strangely missing. Each of the nine boys felt a little guilty, as if he had done something wrong, and, in spite of himself, glanced two or three times at Clem Barnes dressing so quietly in the corner. Each one wanted to say something to Clem, but the words wouldn't come and, anyway, the other fellows were there and what could a fellow say.

The tenth boy, Clem Barnes, felt the unusual quietness, too. But the Negro boy was used to sudden and heavy silences and he went on with his dressing more concerned about basketball than anything in the world right then. Suddenly, however, the room became so still you could have heard a whisper, and Barnes looked up to see Coach Henry Rockwell standing in the doorway.

Rockwell's black eyes were friendly and his thin lips were slanted in that crooked little smile which every boy there knew, and, all at once, everything seemed all right again.

"Hello, boys," Rockwell said softly, "Chet will be along in a few minutes. In the meantime, I'd like to have a little chat with some of you. Bob—"

Two heads jerked up and two pairs of startled eyes flashed wide open. But Rockwell was looking directly at young Bob Blaine and Bob Knox dropped down in his seat like a limp rag.

"Bob," Rockwell continued, "suppose you and Clem, here, go out on the floor and shoot a few baskets. The rest of us will be out in a minute or two."

Rockwell knew boys and liked boys and he particularly liked this group. And the boys in that room knew and liked the Rock. But now, as the boys waited, the eyes which were focused so intently on Rockwell's face were just a bit wary and worried. It was the letter all right. . . . It had to be the letter.

When Bob Blaine and Clem Barnes were gone, Rockwell closed the door and pulled the letter out of his pocket. And when Ralph Hill said he hadn't seen the letter, Rockwell read it all the way through, and then read the names. After a short pause, he began to talk, using "man talk" in straight-from-the-shoulder terms and pulling no punches.

Rockwell told them just about what he had told Chet

Stewart, except that he explained it a little better, maybe. As he talked, the tension disappeared from those tense young faces and a light of understanding came into their eyes. He told them that there was no such thing as a "five-man" team, and the thump, thump, thump, from the gym floor above and the exultant shouts of joy attesting to successful shots brought those eight heads up, and their eyes up, and eight young hopeful All-Americans knew all at once what Coach Rockwell was talking about.

And when the eight boys went out of that dressing room to join Bob Blaine and Clem Barnes for practice, the Little Reds' "starting five" was history and Chet Stewart had himself a TEAM!

The slim crowd which was on hand Friday, January 3, to watch the Little Reds warm-up for their battle with Dulane's Junior Varsity team was back to normal. The old regulars were there, of course. There were a few of the kids' friends, and George and Mrs. Connors, Big Jim Rice and Mrs. Rice, Ralph Hill, Sr. and Mrs. Hill, Jerry Davis, and Prof Blaine. Practically all the older folks were especially anxious to see what Hank Rockwell was going to do about the ridiculous situation into which Chet Stewart had been stupid enough to fall. And they looked curiously at Stewart to see if they could figure out how he felt about all the trouble he had caused.

Ralph Hill, Sr. and Mrs. Hill were particularly interested observers as they watched Chet Stewart because Hillie had acted strangely last night at the dinner table when they had asked him about practice. Each was thinking how difficult it was to understand children nowadays, especially when you did everything in the world for them, like fighting to keep them on the team and spending hours of time every day planning things for them which they never seemed to appreciate, much.

Broad smiles spread across the faces of Ralph Hill, Sr. and Mrs. Hill when, just before the start of the game, Hillie took off his jacket and tossed it on the bench. And two rows ahead of them, big, happy-go-lucky Jim Rice swung around and nodded at Ralph Hill, Sr., and winked knowingly.

But when big, happy-go-lucky Jim Rice turned back to look at the starting five, the smile froze on his face. For the colored boy, Clem Barnes, was standing there without his jacket and, in the little circle gripping hands with Chet Stewart, were Fred Peck, Connie DeWitt, Buddy Connors, and Hillie Hill.

Big, happy-go-lucky Jim Rice's face flushed to a deep purple and he smothered an oath as the sharp elbow of an angry Mrs. Jim Rice poked him in the ribs.

"What's the matter with Teddy, Jim?" she whispered. "He isn't on the starting five! Do you suppose he's sick?"

And just then, just as if he had heard her words, Teddy Rice, turned and smiled up at his father and mother and there was an impish grin on the face of the captain of the Little Reds as he noted the sour expressions on the faces of his father and mother.

At that moment the referee blasted his whistle and the game was on and they sat there amazed at what they saw. For the Little Reds were playing the best basketball of their careers. The amazing part of it was the way they were whipping the ball to the tall, slender, lightning-fast colored boy and the way they slapped him on the back when he scored. A little later, when they looked at the bench, there was Henry Rockwell sitting there watching the Little Reds just as intently as if he were the JV coach.

And just as Jim Rice made up his mind to go down and have a showdown with Henry Rockwell, right then,

Teddy Rice stood up and pulled off his jacket and ran
around the end of the court to the scoring table and reported. Then, their Teddy, already showing signs that
he was going to be a big, happy-go-lucky fellow like
his father, kneeled down in front of the table and
grinned across the floor at them with that impish gleam
in his eyes that his mother could see all that distance
away.

Jim Rice breathed heavily. It was a good thing Rockwell had come along in time to check this nonsense.
Guess that was the reason he was on the bench. What
was the matter with that Stewart?

Then Clem Barnes scored and Teddy trotted out on
the floor and Connie DeWitt said something to Teddy,
then stopped long enough to slap Clem Barnes on the
back before he trotted off the floor. Once again certain
adults who never missed a JV game looked at one another in amazement.

Before they realized it, the game was over and they
saw their kids pounding a tall, shy colored kid on the
back. And they didn't know the Negro boy had just
scored twenty-seven points. So far as that's concerned,
they didn't even know the score of the game. But they
did know that their kids seemed unusually happy about
winning a basketball game.

Some of those who had sat there through all of that
kid game felt as though they had just received a lecture
or been to church; almost as though the kids had been
teaching them something.

Some of those adults sitting there knew what it was
all about . . . knew the score. . . . But there were
others who didn't quite get it and they were still trying to figure it out when the Big Reds came dashing out
on the floor.

CHAPTER 10

ONE-HAND FEVER

Scouting is just as important to the success of a basketball team as it is to a big-league baseball team or to a college football team. In basketball, scouting plays an important part because a good scout can prepare his team to meet particular or peculiar defenses and help them build up a defense for the opponents' style of attack. In addition, the expert basketball scout can carry back to his coach or team important information concerning the other team's individual players.

Coach Henry Rockwell liked to do his own scouting whenever possible. However, high school games in Section Two were usually played on Friday or Saturday nights and, because the Big Reds were usually playing the same night that a future opponent was playing, he often had to rely upon hearsay, past experience, or upon a report tendered by some interested member of the alumni.

There had been no scouting reports on Dulane, and now, as Rockwell sat on the bench and watched the visitors' one-three-one zone completely bottle up the Big Reds' attack, he mentally kicked himself for not sending someone to check up a bit on Dulane's current attack and defense. He looked at the scoreboard. What he saw snapped him into action. The clock showed only five minutes of play remaining in the first half with Dulane leading, 17 to 9.

Rockwell concentrated on the defense the tall visitors were using, his quick, black eyes set to note the slides which the passing of the ball by an attacking team always forces. Such slides are usually the tip-off to the weaknesses of any zone. It was then that Rockwell was aware, for the first time, that the Big Reds were not whipping the ball around the way a good team whips it around against a zone defense.

It wasn't long before he knew why. Todd, Morris, and Schwartz were banging away with one-handers at the goal at every opportunity. The one-hand shots were legitimate according to the chart he had outlined for game shooting, all right, but they weren't good shots. The one-handers usually came after a short dribble and from forced and awkward positions. Rockwell waited until Dulane scored again and then abruptly stood up and waited until Chip saw him and called "Time!"

The Reds formed their huddle near the center line but came hurrying to the bench when Rockwell gestured for them to join him on the side line. As soon as they surrounded him, Rockwell lit into them.

"Start passing that ball around, now, the way you're supposed to be doing. And try a two-one-two attack, Chip, the two-two-one won't work!

"Morris, you and Schwartz handle the ball in the backcourt and Chip, you and Todd take the corners and the sides. Taps, you work across the court from side to side near the free-throw line. Now when someone takes a shot, and I hope it'll be a good shot for a change, I want you, Chip, and you, Todd, and you, Taps, to follow-in every time!

"Come on, now, let's play a little basketball!"

Rockwell had wasted his breath. The situation got no better. It got worse. When the clock showed a little more than two minutes left to play, Rockwell motioned to Stewart and sent him hurrying to the dressing room with orders to have the big blackboard set up so he could do some badly needed between-half chalk-talk work. With a minute left to play, he cleared the bench so there would be no delay in getting the dressing room set up; he didn't want to waste a second of any one of those precious between-half minutes. The bench was hardly cleared before the terrible half ended and the scoreboard showed: Dulane 23, Valley Falls 13.

Surprisingly, as Rockwell hurried the Big Reds ahead of him and down the corridor to the home team dressing room, there was little noise from the home town rooters. Angry as he was, Rockwell caught the significance of the crowd's apathy.

There was a reason for the Valley Falls rooters' unusual behavior tonight and Rockwell knew what it was as well as anyone else. The Big Reds weren't fighting and playing ball and they were going to get beaten! If a team didn't fight and play together it couldn't win, and the Big Reds weren't fighting and they certainly weren't playing together.

"Thirteen points!"

"Ten points behind!"

"And going nowhere fast!"

"Hilton's only scored three points!"

"What's wrong with him, I wonder?"

Chip could have answered that question. A fellow can't score if he doesn't have the ball. And he hadn't got hold of the ball more than six or seven times during the whole half. Dulane's "three-men-in-line" principle was keeping Taps and him and every other Big Red away from the basket.

Rockwell's dressing room procedure was completely outlined and seldom varied. Chip and every other varsity man knew the procedure by heart. The first two minutes you were supposed to rest while Rockwell studied the shot sheets and the scorebook. During those two minutes old Pop Brown, the trainer, bathed your face with a cold towel and pulled your legs straight out in front of you and kept telling you to "Relax, now, relax!"

Then for six straight minutes you got it. During those six minutes the only voice heard in the dressing room was Rock's. And he used the blackboard and the strategy board which was made of metal and was a replica of the basketball court. Five of the little wooden dowels which Rockwell used for men were painted red and five were painted black.

Then there was two minutes of squad discussion. During those two minutes a player could offer suggestions or ask questions. With the minute it took to get to the dressing room and the minute it took to get back to the court, that left three minutes for practice out on the court before the second half began.

But there was no second-half practice tonight. Rock scanned the notes and the scorebook and then went to work on the blackboard. Chip and every player in the room followed the drawings he made on the board.

Rockwell said nothing at all while he was making the drawings, but when he finished, he began to talk.

"The bare outline here on the left shows the way Dulane sets up their zone, assuming the ball is at the point indicated, circle A. Note the three men in line. Players 1, 2, and 3. They try to keep in that formation, but shift with the ball.

"Now get this! This zone is set up so the shifts will keep three men between the ball and the basket at all

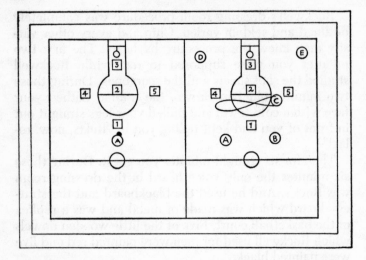

times unless—unless, the ball is passed to a post or to a pivot player. Then they try to double up on him and tie up the ball.

"Now, here on the right side of the board is the attack I want you to set up against it. It's a two-one-two formation. The setup isn't important! It's what you do with it that counts. Now, when you've got it set up, I want you to start passing that ball around or you're sure going to get trimmed!

"Morris, you and Todd will be here in the backcourt, circles A and B. Schwartz, I want you to take Taps' place on the line, here where circle C is shown. And I want you to move as is shown by the flat figure 8 I've drawn there.

"Chip, you will play in the left corner, circle D, and Taps, I want you in the right corner, circle E.

"Now, we'll whip that ball around from one to another and the first thing you know, someone will be

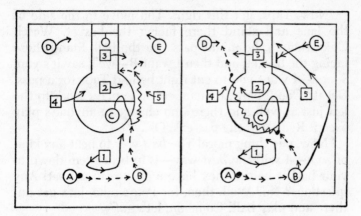

loose for a good shot! Everyone got it? Okay! Now pay attention to these two plays. They'll work!"

Rockwell quickly flipped the board over to the clean side. Then he rapidly sketched in the plays.

"Now, pay attention. You all know where you'll be playing. Watch! A passes to B who passes to C, that's Schwartz. Now, Red, you meet the pass and then dribble hard as shown by the zigzag line. Dulane's 2, 3, and 5, will try to close in on you. Then you'll have the option of passing to D, that'll be Chip, or to E, Taps! Get it?

"Now, on the right side of the board. A passes to B, and again the ball is passed to C, Schwartz. Red, this time you fake a dribble to your left, make it fast, and then dribble to the right, fast and hard. You'll find this time that Dulane's 2, 3, and 4, will try to close in on you, but you'll have a clear pass to Chip, D, and then Chip, you should have a good close-in shot.

"But, Chip, if you can't get a shot away, look here—Look here what Taps and B, that will be either Morris or Todd, have set up there near the right side of the basket.

"Now, Taps, get this right. You move to the side of the lane and stand there facing the basket. Watch Chip, though, he might pass you the ball. Stand there facing the basket, and then I want B—we'll say it's you, Speed—I want you to cut right behind Taps for a pass. Get it? Good! Now, remember, these plays work to the left just as well and there's no change in anyone's play except Red's and the passer's. Okay?

"Now, one thing more! The *best* way to beat any kind of zone—I said the *best* way—is to beat them down to your basket before they have a chance to get set! Any questions? No? Well, then, for Pete's sake, let's get out there and play ball! Come *on*, let's *go!*"

The Big Reds tried, all right. But they didn't have it and couldn't get it. They had lost the touch. The one-hand shots didn't hit, and Dulane, conscious of the tremendous upset they were engineering, played perfect ball. On the offense, they monotonously passed, and passed, and passed, as the minutes wore down, holding on to the ball and trying for a score only when they had a wide-open shot from close range. On the defense all five of them wheeled back under the board and fought like tigers for the ball.

Then the Big Reds became panicky, watching the clock and the scoreboard between passes and shots and defensive play and, just as Joe Kennedy had said in last Sunday's paper, the Big Reds came apart at the seams.

The Big Reds' rooters couldn't believe it as they reluctantly filed out of the darkened gym and they kept looking at the scoreboard still doubting their own eyes and trying to convince themselves that the score was wrong. But it wasn't. And it was still there the last time they looked: Dulane 37, Valley Falls 30.

Down in the dressing room, last year's state champions sat for a long time in front of their lockers and they were all confused and sick at heart.

Chip sat there in that quiet dressing room, hearing nothing except the soft running of water which tinkled thinly in the shower room, and he was thinking of many things. And he sat there and squirmed and turned and shifted his feet and felt the strength well up in his body and hold there because there wasn't anything he could do about it. But it required almost a physical effort to keep from leaping up and dashing back out on that floor to save a game which was already lost. Then he looked at Speed and Red and Taps and he could tell that they felt the same way.

But he didn't look at Buzz because something Buzz had said in one of the huddles had hurt him most of all. *"You mean just because we don't give you the ball so you can take all the shots and make all the points!"*

Chip Hilton didn't look up any more that night nor the next day at the Sugar Bowl. And on Sunday he never once looked at the papers but studied most of the day in his room and his heart was heavy and sore. Sunday evening, when his mother and T. A. K. Baxter were enjoying a cold snack, Chip went down into the cellar to the laboratory because it was the quietest place in the house and he needed to be alone so he could think.

There he found the water dripping from the tap in the sink and some cigarette ashes beside the filing cabinet. He noticed those things, but his mind was too troubled to pay much attention, for nothing mattered right then except the big barrier which was building up each day between all the fellows.

CHAPTER 11

JUNIOR VARSITY STARS

HENRY ROCKWELL had spent a gloomy week end and nothing had happened today to lift his spirit of depression. He swung around in the big, leather chair, which had followed him from the dingy office he had occupied in the old Central School to this book- and picture-lined private office he now called his own in this modern high school building, and gazed out the window and across and beyond Ohlsen Stadium.

Rockwell wasn't worried because his team had lost a game. Long ago he had learned that "you can't win them all!" But the veteran mentor was much concerned about his team's steady decline in team play and spirit. That was an athletic disease similar to cancer. It was hard to define and difficult to cure.

This team was dropping like a plummet down the side of a building and he knew he had to do something about it—quick. The success of the entire season hinged upon the results of the next four or five games. Maybe the next two games. If this team went into a real tail spin, he'd have to be prepared to do something drastic. But what?

Rockwell sat in the comfortable chair for a long time,

staring at the blue sky which stretched miles on end across the valley, and then he turned abruptly back to his desk and picked up another anonymous letter which had come in the mail that day. Muttering something uncomplimentary about the cowardly writer and crumpling up the sheet of paper, he made a neat two-pointer in the wastebasket in the corner.

But something in that anonymous letter had aroused Rockwell's liking for a good fight. A few minutes later Chet Stewart and the JV's were surprised to receive the second visit from Coach Rockwell in less than a week. Rockwell rarely trespassed upon his assistant's practice periods and seldom called upon the Little Reds for a scrimmage against the varsity, because it was no contest and not of much benefit to either team.

Today Rockwell smiled at the group of youngsters who were standing quietly waiting for him to speak.

"You fellows feel real tough this afternoon?"

They nodded eagerly and Captain Teddy Rice voiced their feelings. "Yes, sir. Almost rough enough to trim the varsity!"

Rockwell nodded his head approvingly. "That's what I wanted to hear," he said abruptly. "Chet, bring 'em over to the gym at four thirty!"

Pop Brown, Valley Falls' veteran trainer, was about the only cheerful person in the Big Reds' dressing room that afternoon. And he tried to raise the spirits of the boys who were dressing so slowly and quietly.

"Look here, now," he said, stopping directly in front of Chip. "Look here— Just because you all had a bad night against those Dulane boys ain't no reason for to forget there's other games acomin'! Heck, one game ain't agoin' to stop us, no sir!"

Chip smiled weakly. "You're right, Pop," he said, squaring his jaw. "That'll be the last one!"

Soapy Smith had been unusually quiet. And when Soapy was quiet in a dressing room or anywhere else, things were bad. Now he tried to help Pop cheer up his teammates. "Aw, come on you guys," he said pleadingly. "Let's snap out of it! We've got that one out of our system and now we can really burn a trail!"

But it was wasted effort. The Big Reds were down. Way down.

A little later, up on the court and right after the warm-up drill, the JV's came walking out on the south end of the court.

Soapy Smith got a kick out of that. "Look," he growled, "just what I need—some fresh meat!"

It was "fresh meat" all right. The JV's were up and the varsity took it too easy and the Little Reds fought the "big team" to a standstill. Stewart had matched Clem against Chip and, much as Chip wanted to help Clem, he didn't take it easy. He gave Clem a rough time. But then Chip Hilton could give any player in the state a rough time.

When Rockwell's whistle and "That's all," ended the scrimmage, everyone on the varsity was surprised to see him check the JV's and ask Teddy Rice, Fred Peck, and Clem Barnes to remain behind.

"Now, what's he up to?" Soapy growled.

They found out the next night, for those three boys were the first players out on the floor for varsity practice. They were embarrassed, and a bit scared, but proud to be there—on the varsity!

The Valley Falls state champions knew the Rock and knew most of his tricks. They got a kick out of this bit of musty coaching strategy that he was using to scare them into his way of thinking.

"The old goat think we're going to fall for that?" Soapy chuckled.

So all that week the Big Reds exchanged winks and sly smiles as Rockwell tried first Teddy Rice, and then Fred Peck, and finally Clem Barnes in a varsity position. And in spite of their knowledge of Rock's methods, the Big Reds poured it on each of the newcomers. Rockwell got a kick out of the practices, too, for the varsity was doing exactly what he wanted them to do. He wanted to see if the kids could take it.

The kids showed they could take it, all right, and give it, too. Teddy Rice, captain of the JV team, was five feet eight inches in height and one hundred and fifty pounds of fighting fury. A fellow watching him play for five minutes could tell why the blond, blue-eyed kid with the crew haircut had been elected captain of the Little Reds; he didn't know when to quit.

Fred Peck was five feet ten inches in height and weighed around one hundred and sixty. He looked and moved a lot like Speed Morris. Maybe not quite so fast, but with the same drive. The dark-complexioned kid was a fine dribbler, a good rebounder, and showed signs of being a good backcourt operator.

Clem Barnes was six feet one inch in height. But there all comparison with his JV teammates ended. Clem was extremely slender, but his muscles were long and he was wiry and moved with deceptive speed. One look at his long arms and big hands and the ease with which he handled a basketball told you the story on Clem Barnes. He was a natural.

So the three kids took all the Big Reds could give and came back for more. And as each one played, the other two sat on the bench and rooted for him. Before the week was over, the kids were no longer JV's but Big Reds, and the older boys, with the exception of Buzz Todd, moved over and made room for them on the varsity squad.

Buzz Todd carried the hazing a bit too far with Clem Barnes, but Clem never indicated in any way that he was aware of Todd's persecution. He just kept playing and looking better until you could see the respect in the eyes of Speed and Red and Soapy and Taps increase every day.

Chip got a surprise Wednesday, for Pop Brown told him not to dress when he arrived for practice. "Mr. Rock wants to see you in his office, Chipper. Go on up."

Chip paused outside Rockwell's office. Now what?

Chip had been in that office a great number of times in the past three years and he knew a lot about it. Yet, each time he visited it, he was thrilled by the pictures which hung on the walls and by the rows of sports and record books which reposed in the bookcases.

When Chip knocked and entered, Rockwell jumped up and grabbed his hat and overcoat. "You ready?" he asked, smiling.

Chip was confused. "I, I—"

"Don't worry about it! We're going on a little drive this afternoon, you and I. No practice for us. We're going over to Delford on a little scouting expedition. You know what's going on over there, don't you?"

Chip knew that all right. Delford was tangling with Southern and he'd sure like to see that game, but he had to work. . . .

Rockwell knew what Chip was thinking about. "No work for you tonight, either. I called your boss and he said it would be all right 'if we could win Friday night at Southern.'"

Chip enjoyed the drive to Delford because Rockwell didn't talk too much and, when he did, it wasn't about basketball. Rockwell knew boys and he knew that his team's captain was just as concerned about the team as he was.

Any time you played at Delford you were in for a hot evening. What the team might lack in ability it made up in fight. And tonight was a red-letter evening. Southern was leading Section Two and Delford had its best team in years.

Southern was a junior team. The previous year Russell Whitcomb had decided to rebuild his team and had placed five sophomores on the starting five. The kids had started slowly and then had caught fire and had burned up the league. In fact, the kids had barely missed a bid to the state championships.

Back intact this year, they had won eight in a row and were looking better every game they played. But winning at Delford was a tough assignment no matter how good you were, and when the teams lined up for the center jump and you noticed the matching of the players, it was easy to see that the Southerners lacked the height and weight to compete with Red Henry and his tall teammates. The only exception was the Southerner's captain, a stocky, six-footer with a square jaw and big, sloping shoulders.

"Hey, Whitcomb, that your JV team?"

"Where'd you get those scarecrows?"

"Past those kids' bedtime. Take 'em home!"

"We'll chase 'em home!"

But they didn't chase those kids home. They were fast and clever and they were fighters. And the best fighter on the floor was the Southern captain, Bill Berrien, a fighting rebel who dominated the defensive backboard as though he owned it. Slowly but surely, the Southern kids crawled out in front and stayed there. In the third quarter, Southern's tall, slender center fouled out and the Delford rooters took hope. Red Henry was six six, and Berrien, who switched over to the center spot, was only a little guy, or so it seemed.

"Now you got 'em, Red!"

"Give the ball to Red!"

But Bill Berrien was fast and strong and he liked it rough. When Henry tried to push him around, the Southern captain really went to work.

Chip was busy making notes on the individual Southern players and Rockwell was concentrating on the kids' offense and defense. But Chip couldn't help marveling at the fight and hustle of the Southern captain. He was faking and feinting and dribbling around Henry as though he were standing still on the offense and, on the defense, Berrien played in front of Henry, on the sides, and seemed to know just where Henry was weakest.

With two minutes to go, Southern led by three points and the game degenerated into a dogfight. But the kids fought like champions and won the grudging admiration of the home crowd by lasting it out to win 46 to 41.

While Chip and Coach Rockwell were scouting Southern at Delford, Valley Falls town fans were getting another dose of fire department basketball. The Independents used the Y gym for their games, except for special attractions. Tonight the opposition was the Clinton Big Five and the game was being played at the Y.

John Schroeder, Doc Jones, little Paddy Jackson, and about every dyed-in-the-wool fan in town was there, not to mention the Big Red varsity and the JV's. It was a good show, all right, all the more so, perhaps, because the floor was small and, under T. A. K. Baxter's system, a fellow could shoot from any spot on the floor. And that is exactly what the Independents did! They shot away as soon as they got the ball and then banged in after the rebound, running the visitors dizzy. It was no contest.

The Clinton Big Five was made up of former high school and a few college players who had slowed down, and they didn't have a chance to cope with Baxter's slam-bang, racehorse style of play.

Speed Morris, Buzz Todd, Soapy Smith, and Red Schwartz were sitting together in the last row of seats high up by the windows and what they saw didn't improve their frame of mind. They looked down at Baxter substituting freely now that his charges were out in front by thirty points, and though no one would put the wish into words, each of the high school players wondered what it would be like if Baxter were coaching them. It would really be something to score twenty or thirty points a game all by yourself!

T. A. K. Baxter was riding the crest of the wave. The sports news he was giving to Pete Williams and Joe Kennedy had drawn them into his corner. They wanted to give this colorful stranger all the publicity they could, for he was news. They didn't overlook his pottery background, either, because local readers ate up anything and everything you printed about basketball and pottery.

Baxter was just about ready to spring his carefully baited trap on J. P. Ohlsen. He had the formulas all set, but he needed those five little pieces of pottery which were down in the cellar of the Hilton home. They represented the kind of ware he wanted Ohlsen to think he had produced with domestic clay and his secret formulas, "T. A. K."

But there was still a bug in his plan. He knew that scarcely a day passed that the Hilton kid did not spend a few minutes in the laboratory in the cellar and Baxter knew Chip would surely miss the five pieces of ware that were sitting in plain view on the workbench.

So Baxter, working carefully, had made a rough copy

of one of the pieces of ware. But it wasn't good and he had fearfully substituted it for one of Chip's priceless pieces and had put it behind the others, hoping Chip would not examine it too carefully.

Now, as Baxter sat on the Independents' bench, he kept looking at his watch. He wanted to be sure he would have time to run out to the Hilton's and pick up the bag which had the priceless piece of pottery carefully packed inside, and catch the eleven-thirty train. He knew a place where he could have five duplicates made, and then he could substitute them for Bill Hilton's beautiful work and arrange for a business session with J. P. Ohlsen.

On the way home, Chip and Rockwell talked over the game and the fine Southern team they were to meet at Southern Friday night.

"They're good, Chip," Rockwell commented. "Very good! And we'll have to be better than we've been for a long time if we're going to take 'em."

Nothing was said then for a long stretch of snow-lined road. These two friends, just about as close as coach and player can get, sat there wondering and worrying about the Big Reds and what had happened to them. Later Chip's thoughts swung around to Baxter and the fire department basketball which had caught hold in Valley Falls and he cautiously asked Rockwell if he had known of Baxter when he was at State.

"No, Chip," Rockwell said thoughtfully, "I don't ever remember hearing about him up there. Why?"

"Oh, I don't know, Coach, except that I couldn't find anything about him in Dad's old scrapbooks and I was just wondering—"

Rockwell had never met Baxter, but he hadn't missed any of the write-ups about the Independents and their new style of play. And he certainly hadn't failed to get the significance of the little pot shots Kennedy and Williams had been taking at him in the papers. Furthermore, he knew that Baxter was supposed to have known Chip's father and that he had moved into the Hilton home. And he knew this boy well enough to know that Chip Hilton was particularly worried about that.

"I understand he was supposed to have played there, Chip," Rockwell said slowly. "Would you like me to find out more about him."

Chip didn't answer that question right away. He wanted to think it over. It seemed to him a little like spying on someone, but he thought of his mother and suddenly he decided to let Rockwell help him clear up his doubts.

"Coach," he said hesitantly, "could you find out if Mr. Baxter really went to State? I mean about the time my father did?"

"Why, sure, Chip. That's easy. I'll call tomorrow."

When Rockwell dropped Chip off at the Hilton home it was midnight, but Mary Hilton was waiting up for him.

"Did you have a nice time, Chip?"

"I sure did, Mother. A swell time! Southern won and that's bad news for us Friday night. How did the Independents make out?"

"Oh, they won by a big score. A hundred and three to something—Mr. Baxter was telling me about it before he left."

"Left?"

"Yes, he was called out of town and left on the eleven thirty for Chicago."

"He coming back?"

"Oh, yes. He said he wouldn't be finished here for another two or three weeks. There was a big article about him in the paper tonight. On the front page. He's leaving for England around the first of February—Where did I put that paper? Here it is, read it."

About that time, Mr. T. A. K. Baxter, self-styled author and leading authority on American pottery, was sitting in the club car of the midnight express bound for Chicago. He sat there looking out the window at the shadowy landscape and his mind was deeply concerned with his plan. This little trip was going to cut heavily into the balance of his bankroll. But the thing had to go through, now, or he'd be in a pretty kettle of fish.

He thought of that one little piece of ware he had worked so laboriously to make and, for a moment, he was disturbed by thoughts of what would happen if the kid happened to get hold of it and examine it closely. But it was too late now to do anything but hope for the best. It was all in the lap of the gods and with good luck he'd be back in Valley Falls the first of the week with five little substitute pieces of pottery which he needed so badly to make his plan foolproof. The substitutes wouldn't have to be perfect, but they'd have to be passable.

The kid had probably handled those five pieces of ware a hundred times and he wasn't a chump when it came to pottery, even if he was only a kid.

CHAPTER 12

MOUNTAIN OR MOLEHILL

SOUTHERN was located in the extreme southern part of Section Two and straddled the river which separated the two states. The first settler and the store at the fording point on the river, and eventually the post office which was housed in the store, had remained on the north side of the river and that was why the town of Southern was in the state and in Section Two. The residents were, for the most part, retired farmers from across the river and those who followed the usual trade and businesses to be found in a river town.

It was a sleepy town most of the time. In the summer it got extremely hot in the afternoons and that was reason enough for a pleasant siesta. In the winters, the slowness of the river traffic was a good excuse to hibernate. As is usual in a river town on the southern border, practically all of the heavy work on the docks, loading, unloading, and carrying, was performed by Negro laborers.

But Southern wasn't sleepy this winter. And the reason was Southern's high school varsity basketball team. The five kids comprising the starting team had played together through grade school, in the first year of high

105

school, and then, last year, had played intact as Southern's varsity. They had played like champions, too. After a shaky start, they had come strong in the last half of the season losing to the Big Reds at Valley Falls, 44 to 45, but beating Steeltown a week later 36 to 32 to put the Iron Men out of the running for Section Two honors, thus moving Valley Falls into the runner-up position behind Weston. That had given Valley Falls a chance to play in the All-State tournament at University and the Big Reds had come through to win the state championship.

The Big Reds left Valley Falls Friday afternoon at two o'clock and the three-hour bus trip brought them to the Southern Hotel at exactly five o'clock, just as Prof Rogers had advised the manager of the hotel in his letter making the reservations. They had stopped on the way for a brief meal as per their usual custom and after their two-hour nap would be ready for the game. After the game, they'd have their meal and then a long walk and permission to break training by remaining up until midnight.

Rockwell was the last person off the bus and stopped to chat with the driver. Prof Rogers, Chet Stewart, and the manager, Biggie Cohen, were responsible for all arrangements such as assigning the boys to their rooms. So Rockwell was surprised when he entered the lobby to see the boys standing around in little groups and Rogers and Stewart engaged in earnest conversation with the clerk at the desk. Biggie Cohen was standing near by with a piece of paper listing the room pairings of the boys. Rockwell sensed something was wrong and he had an idea that it might have something to do with Pop Brown and Clem Barnes. But his approach to the desk was unhurried and his voice was calm when he addressed Rogers.

"What's the trouble, Prof? Didn't they get our reservations?"

"Why, yes, Hank. But something's come up and the manager wants to see us in his office in the mezzanine."

Rockwell looked keenly at Rogers and then at the clerk behind the desk before following Rogers up the steps to the mezzanine and the office of the manager.

"What is it, Prof? Barnes?"

Rogers nodded soberly. "That's it, Hank."

The manager of the Southern Hotel had been in the hotel business for many years and he knew how to handle people. His keen eyes evaled the two teachers quickly and he extended his hand and greeted them like long-lost brothers and his smile was as broad as the Mississippi River.

"Gentlemen, my name is Hankins. Everybody calls me George. Glad to meet you, er, Mr. Rogers, and er, Coach Rockwell. Sit down, gentlemen. Hope you had a nice trip down. Well, you fellows had better be good. These kids of ours are red-hot!"

Prof Rogers cleared his throat and managed to interpose, "We're hav—"

Hankins nodded his head and kept right on going. "Now, er, Mr. Rogers, I'm in a sort of a predicament. We're jammed up here with a lot of unexpected business and— Now, don't worry, we got your reservations, all right, and we'll be able to take care of most of your party, all right, but we'd like to send a couple of you over to a little place we have for just such emergencies. I'm sure you can understand how it is in the hotel business."

Hankins looked at them expectantly, but when there was no response he continued amiably, "Now, there's a nice place right around the corner, almost, where the two colored gentlemen can stay. It's a nice place. In fact, we've already called them and made arrangements." He turned to a young man sitting at a small desk.

"Bill, why don't you go down to the desk and get the boys straightened out. You might send Catlin over to Byrds with the other two gentlemen."

Rockwell leaned forward in his chair and looked the manager straight in the eyes. Then he spoke softly but with a bit of a rasp in his voice. "Are you trying to tell us, Mr. Hankins, that the two colored persons in our party will have to go somewhere else?"

Hankins nodded his head and smiled. "That's it, Coach. I'm glad you understand the problem. You know how the people feel about such things down in this end of the state."

Rockwell stood up slowly and shook his head. "No," he said softly, "I don't know how people feel about such things down in this end of the state. I only know that we have a party of seventeen persons and that we always travel together. We never break up our groups when we travel." He turned to Rogers.

"Didn't you advise Mr. Hankins by letter that there would be seventeen in our party, Prof?"

"I sure did, Rock."

Hankins was on his feet now, aware for the first time that this matter might not be so easily handled as he had thought. "Now, er, look here, Coach. We got the letter, all right, and it said a party of seventeen, all right. But we never dreamed that there would be two colored persons in the party. Down here we have a different situation than you have a little farther north.

"You see, down here, the colored people have their own schools and hotels and restaurants and— Why, they even have their own private swimming pools and beaches and everything—"

Rockwell interrupted the voluble manager with a wave of his hand. "That's all right, Mr. Hankins," he said coolly. "Isn't there another hotel in this town where we can stop?"

"Oh, now, Coach, that's not the attitude to take. Why, your teams have been stopping here for years. We're proud to have you high school groups stopping here at the Southern and we don't want to disappoint you in any way. There isn't another hotel in town, sorry to say, and er, I tell you what— I'll call Coach Whitcomb at the high school."

While Hankins' secretary was calling the high school, the manager was telling Rockwell how badly he felt about the matter and this was the first time he'd ever met the problem and hotel business was sure a trying field. Then he got Russell Whitcomb, Southern's coach, on the telephone and Whitcomb said he'd be there in five minutes.

Rockwell waited in the office scarcely hearing Hankins while Rogers went downstairs, at Rockwell's suggestion, to join Chet Stewart and take the boys for a fifteen-minute walk.

Coach Henry Rockwell was a perfectionist in his coaching, and every detail which was concerned with his basketball team was important. His coaching went beyond the basketball court and that was one of the big reasons for his success down through the years. The veteran coach expected his boys to conduct themselves like gentlemen in their off-court behavior at home or on the road.

Cleanliness and neatness was a fetish with the veteran coach and Valley Falls' athletes learned early in their athletic careers that it was wise to take pride in their personal appearance. The group of boys who lounged about the lobby were neat in appearance and mannerly in deportment and would have been a credit to any school. Yet, as they stood in little groups, talking and laughing, you could detect the nervousness in their bearing. They were ill at ease because every one of them knew that this delay in Rockwell's regular trip routine was unusual. And they knew why.

Each boy tried to act nonchalant, and as if it were customary to loaf around a hotel lobby before checking in and being assigned to his room. Biggie Cohen went from one player to the next ostensibly making up the room pairings that he already knew by heart and Chet Stewart corraled the JV's and began quizzing them on some of his basketball principles.

Pop Brown and Clem Barnes were busily engaged in the study of a large painting which hung over the lobby fireplace but which neither really saw.

When Rogers came down from the mezzanine and suggested they take a ten or fifteen minute hike "to loosen up their legs after the long ride," everyone was relieved. But this, too, was a departure from the regular procedure and much as they tried to be their usual selves it was impossible. They straggled slowly along on the walk, and when they neared the hotel coming back, every person in that little group unconsciously slowed down his steps and reluctantly entered the lobby.

Not long after Rogers left Hankins' office, Whitcomb came hurrying in, panting and obviously disturbed. He had gleaned only an inkling of the difficulty over the telephone, but he knew exactly what Rockwell was up against, and one glance at the Valley Falls coach's tense face was enough to tell him the problem Hankins had on his hands.

"Russ" Whitcomb was a pleasant-faced, friendly man in his late thirties. This was his third year as head coach at Southern and he had been remarkably successful in football as well as basketball. He was extremely concerned, now, because he admired Rockwell very much and he wanted to keep his friendship. The warmth of his greeting to Rockwell did not escape Hankins, and while the two coaches conversed in low tones the worried manager considered the problem from all angles.

Hankins was thinking that maybe he could work this out, someway. The Valley Falls outfit would only be here the one night and they were leaving early in the morning. He had already set up a special dining room for them. Maybe the smartest thing would be to assign rooms to them and hope for the best.

Russ Whitcomb and Rockwell were both relieved when Hankins abruptly announced, "Maybe we're making a mountain out of a molehill. We'll let it go, Russ, this time. I'll call downstairs and tell them to forget about it.

"Coach, you come with me and I'll get you a good room, myself."

The two coaches followed Hankins, but there was little respect in Rockwell's eyes nor in his heart for this man. Rockwell had no use for any man who bent with the wind no matter from which direction it blew.

While Rockwell was unpacking his suitcase, Whitcomb sat in a chair by the window trying to figure out a way to approach the Valley Falls coach with the problem which was facing them both because of Clem Barnes. Rockwell seemed to take it for granted that everything was all right now that the hotel situation had been cleared. But Whitcomb knew it was just the beginning.

"Rock," he said worriedly, "I don't know what we're going to do about the Negro boy when it comes to dressing, tonight. You know, they don't let Negro boys play against white boys down here.

"You see, Rock, unlike some towns down this way, we take pretty good care of our colored folks. They have their own high school and shows and hotels and everything.

"And the people down here just can't understand why the people in the North and in the East seem so much concerned with the problem.

"Rock, that feeling has come down through the years and the generations and it has come right down to the kids, too. You'll see the white boys and the Negro boys talking together and friendly like, but the grown folks just wouldn't stand for mixed teams!"

Rockwell listened quietly. He knew Russ Whitcomb to be a swell fellow. Sincere, thoughtful, courteous, and fair in his thinking. And as Rockwell looked at the young coach, his mouth slanted in that friendly, crooked smile of his. "Russ," he said softly, "I understand your position. You see, I grew up below the Mason-Dixon line and spent most of my kid school life in the South. Not in the deep South, understand, but enough South to understand how some folks feel and think about race discrimination.

"But there's another side to the question. Valley Falls has no special school for colored boys and girls. And as regular students in our school system they're entitled to all the privileges and honors the school offers. This Barnes kid has shown he is a good enough basketball player to be worthy of a place on our squad, maybe on our first team, and, well, he's got to go where the team goes and play where they play.

"By the way, Russ, what happened when you played Steeltown? What about *their* Negro boy? What about Minor?"

"He didn't play here, Rock. We played football and basketball against him at Steeltown and the kids didn't think much about it, but we had a sort of gentleman's agreement about him playing here. So they didn't even bring him along.

"Gosh, Rock, they'd run me out of town if I used a Negro boy. Of course, that's impossible because there's none in the school, but even if there was, I wouldn't dare to use him. Why, one time I arranged a scrimmage with the Negro high school and some of the people in town raised such a fuss when they heard about it that I thought sure I was going to be fired. Some of the members of the school board made a point of telling me specifically that the next time I pulled a stunt like that my job here in Southern would be taken away."

Rockwell nodded his head understandingly. "I've heard of that kind of deal, Russ, but I wouldn't cheapen myself by being a party to any agreements like the one you mentioned, and I don't believe anyone who considers himself a gentleman would, either. No, sir!"

The problem was too much for Whitcomb and he sat there trying desperately to figure a way out of the predicament. After a short pause, he snapped his fingers. He knew someone who might know the answer.

"Tell you what, Rock," Whitcomb said, "suppose I call Murtagh. He's the principal. Great guy! We'll go over to his office."

Half an hour later, after making sure the boys were all in bed, Rockwell met the principal of Southern's high school, T. R. Murtagh. Murtagh was a pleasant-faced gentleman in his fifties. He listened soberly and understandingly as Whitcomb told him what had happened at the hotel and how Rockwell felt about Clem Barnes.

"Rock says he'd rather forfeit the game and go home, T. R., and well—" Whitcomb looked at Murtagh hopefully and continued, "Well, that's why we're here. I don't know what to do."

As Russ Whitcomb talked, Murtagh's expression grew more serious, and when he finally spoke his voice expressed deep concern.

"Russ is right, Coach. The problem is a serious one."

Murtagh paused and the silence was deep and heavy. Then in a thoughtful voice the principal continued: "A Negro boy never has played against a white boy in a basketball game in our high school, but I suppose there has to be a first time or at least an attempted first time. Personally, I don't know of any better time than tonight to see just how deep the prejudice is in this town. The citizens of Southern are keenly interested in this fine basketball team of ours, and if Russ, here, can control his players, I don't see why we shouldn't let the boy dress and see what happens.

"Certainly, if tolerance is to be found anywhere, it should be found in the hearts of those who believe in sportsmanship and the value of sports as an educational force in our schools.

"We must keep in mind that this is a serious step. I am not sure we are not treading upon quicksand. However, I am willing to do my part and, if you are willing to go along, Russ— Well, then, let's face the thing. Personally, I won't mind doing a little searching for a new job if we can cause a few people with prejudice-filled hearts to do a little soul-searching—"

All this time the Valley Falls coach had said not a word. He had been watching the two Southern teachers and his face clearly showed his admiration for their courageous decision. Without a word Rockwell got to his feet and shook hands with Principal Murtagh. However the game came out tonight, win, lose, or draw, here was a man he could respect.

CHAPTER 13

SOUTHERN EXPOSURE

T. R. MURTAGH knew what he was talking about, all right. The citizens of Southern were very much awake and aware of the championship potentialities of their kids—their kids who had narrowly missed the state tournament last year and who were tearing Section Two apart this year. . . .

"Yep, the kids have won nine in a row!"

"And they haven't even been pressed, yet!"

"Valley Falls knocked us out of the race last year!"

"Yeah, we'll pay 'em back for that—tonight!"

"Rockwell better not use a zone tonight!"

"He's foxy, that old guy!"

"Lucky, you mean!"

"Best coach in the state!"

"Could be, but we've got the best team in the state!"

"You can say that again!"

When the preliminary game ended with the Southern JV's trimming Valley Falls' Little Reds by a score of 31 to 12, the joy of the Southerners was expressed in a cheering thunder which could be heard blocks away. Of course, they didn't know that Fred Peck and Ted Rice and Clem Barnes had been "upped" to the varsity and that without the help of these three the Valley Falls JV's were pretty hopeless indeed.

The veteran Big Reds knew it. And there was a smoldering resentment in the hearts of some of them against the three boys who had "run out" on their teammates just to sit on the varsity bench. And when they trotted out on the floor for the warm-up, they were a little bitter toward Rock, and Chet, and even Old Pop who had made such a fuss over the new additions to the varsity squad.

The Southern fans greeted the Big Reds with a burst of applause. This fan-jammed gymnasium was a tribute to the champions of the state. This was the game every person in Southern had been waiting for.

The Big Reds went right into their three-lane warm-up drill and, as the boys cut under the basket for the pass, the shot, the rebound and the hard, fast pass back to the center, the applause suddenly died down to a whisper.

Then you heard the whispers, and the muttering and the rumble which grew and grew.

"Can't be!"

"Yes it is! I ought to know!"

"*Sure* he's a Negro!"

Then, when the awareness of Clem Barnes had changed from questioning appraisal to a growing certainty that the tall, slender boy with the dark skin was indeed a Negro, a murmur started and grew and grew until it sounded like a freight train roaring around the bend.

"Can't be! But it is!"

"Never heard of such a thing!"

"Heard of it, but I never thought I'd see it!"

"Me either! At least not in our own high school!"

"Our kids won't play against him!"

Henry Rockwell sat on the bench to the right of the scorer's table and his ears burned and his heart fluttered and pressed high up in his chest until there was a growing pain right under the knot in his tie and he had a tough time breathing. And his mind was in a turmoil and he wished now that he had taken his team back to Valley Falls that afternoon.

Then Rockwell began to worry about the kids he had brought down here and the pain in his chest was replaced by a burning anger.

Just then, fortunately, the Southern kids came dashing out on the floor and the rooters got up on their feet and lifted the roof. These were their kids! The next state champions! The kids that were putting Southern on the map!

The Southern band and the cheering squad went into action, and most of the people there put thoughts of the colored boy on the Valley Falls squad out of their minds as they cheered their kids to the skies.

But there were some who continued to murmur and talk about the Negro boy and wonder whether or not he was a regular on the Valley Falls team and wonder what would happen if "that Rockwell" tried to use him against their kids. And there were a few "sportsmen" sitting in the bleachers near the floor at the end of the court where the Big Reds were warming up and they made some remarks which no true sportsman would ever make.

Clem Barnes heard some of these remarks and he tried to concentrate on the warm-up drill, but he was new to the squad and he had a lot of things on his mind. He got butter-fingered and he missed a couple of passes and he missed the basket and the laughter and the booing that followed the missed shot made things worse.

The Big Reds heard the jeers and the catcalls and the

things which were being said and some of them began to get mad. Chip Hilton slapped Clem on the back and said, "Come on! Snap out of it!"

It was a good thing that right then Rockwell signaled them and they all left the floor for the dressing room. Southern went down to their dressing room at the same time and, in the interim, the Southern cheering squad and the band went to work and the crowd didn't have much chance to do anything but cheer.

A minute later the two teams came dashing out on the floor and the cheering broke loose again. Those rooters who were more concerned with thoughts of Clem Barnes than they were with the game were drowned out by the thundering roar. The "fans" who had directed the scurrilous remarks toward Clem Barnes were temporarily stilled because the Negro boy was sitting on the bench and the starting five for the Valley Falls Big Reds was the one they had been reading about in the papers.

Captain Chip Hilton and Red Schwartz were at the forwards, Taps Browning at center, and Speed Morris and Buzz Todd were at the guards. The Southern lineup was the same which had breezed through nine straight games. Captain Bill Berrien was shaking hands with Chip Hilton, and Bob Ford was smiling at Taps Browning, the tops of their heads even at six feet six inches from the floor. Little Buddy Glasco was gripping hands with Buzz Todd, and Rip Kimmel had grabbed Speed Morris by the arm and they were slapping each other on the back because they had played against each other the year before and knew and respected each other's ability. Gil Lydon and Red Schwartz, evenly matched as to height and build, were pulling at one another's hands just as they had a year ago, and both were thinking the same thing, "I *would* draw you!"

Then they were all standing and reciting the "Salute to the Flag" in unison and then the whistle sounded and the game was on.

Ford outjumped Taps and it was Southern's ball. Chip immediately switched over and picked up Kimmel, Speed Morris took Gil Lydon, and Red Schwartz checked Bill Berrien. Chip knew he would have his hands full with Kimmel. Kimmel could hit from outside with long, two-hand set shots, was expert at driving around his guard if he was played tight, and, once within fifteen feet of the basket, was deadly with a running one-hander.

Chip played him as close as he dared, but Kimmel got a long set away and it never touched the rim as it swished through for the first score of the game. The crowd ate that up. Kimmel had put that Hilton kid in his place.

"Hey, Hilton! Having trouble?"

"Bet he matches that twenty-six on your shirt tonight!"

Chip heard some of those taunts as he broke down court. Bill Berrien dropped over in front of Chip, pointing and yelling, "I've got Hilton! Take Schwartz, Kim!"

Chip spurted and beat Berrien in to the basket, but it was wasted effort. When he pivoted around and looked for the ball he was just in time to see Buzz Todd dribble to the right-hand corner and let a one-hander fly at the basket.

Right then, Chip's respect for Bill Berrien went up fifty per cent. Berrien faced the basket, and blocked him expertly away from the rebound. When Chip sidestepped to the left, Berrien shifted swiftly and surely and there he was again, between Chip and the backboard. Then, he leaped high in the air with perfect timing, grasped the ball with one hand, and threw it hard and true down the left side line to the five-foot two-inch Glasco.

Glasco was off like a shot, dribbling around and past Todd as if Buzz was nailed to the floor. Morris, dropping back with his eyes glued on Lydon, took after Glasco a second too late, catching the little dribbler just short of the basket. But Speed couldn't stop the shot and Southern was out in front, 4 to 0, in less than a minute of play.

Speed grabbed the ball just as it dropped through the net, stepped out of bounds, and fired a hard baseball pass right back up court to Todd. Buzz pivoted around with the ball, dribbled into the one-hand shooting area, and let fly with another running one-hander.

Chip followed-in, but Bill Berrien was right there between him and the basket again, blocking him out and taking the rebound. And that was the way it went, Berrien controlling the Big Reds' rebounds and starting the Southern quick-break rolling each time with a perfect catcher's peg far down the court. At the end of the quarter, Southern was out in front, 14 to 3. Speed had hit with a one-hander and Chip had dropped in a free throw when Berrien had body-blocked him away from the basket.

The crowd had liked that because Berrien was tying Chip in a knot, blocking him away from the basket time after time. So far the Big Reds had shown no offense whatever. It had been up the floor and let it fly. At the half, the score was: Southern 23, Valley Falls 9.

Rockwell's dressing-room talk was fiery and bitter and it sent the Big Reds out on the court fighting mad. But it didn't mean a thing. Southern took up where they had left off and, at the end of the third quarter, they were out in front, 34 to 18.

Something happened right then at the start of the fourth period which was indicative of the collapse of the Big Reds. Schwartz and Todd nearly came to blows when Red called Buzz a "heaver." Todd came right back and accused Schwartz of "hogging the ball," and Chip called "Time!"

Rockwell took care of that by sending Soapy Smith in for Schwartz and little Lefty Peters for Todd. The substitution seemed to give the Big Reds a "shot in the arm," for Chip got the ball for a change and earned himself six quick points and a resounding hand of applause by getting away from Berrien three times in a row. Then Southern called for a time-out. So with five minutes to go the score was: Southern 34, Valley Falls 24.

But when play was resumed, Glasco turned on the heat and scored twice in fifty seconds, faking Peters out of position and dribbling in for easy lay-up shots. Chip called "Time" again and the Big Reds huddled in front of Rockwell. The continuous roar from the crowd had clearly indicated their feelings with respect to the superiority their kids were showing in this important game with the state champions. And while they were "riding" the Big Reds and cheering their kids to the rafters, Rockwell had been thinking about Clem Barnes, mentally debating the advisability of sending him into this game.

A feeling of caution held him back for an instant and then he remembered his words to Chet Stewart. "The best player gets the job." That did it! Rockwell knew that in this spot, at any other time, and any other place, he would have substituted Barnes for Peters. And he didn't hesitate another second. He turned and almost lifted Barnes to his feet.

"In for Peters, Clem," he said sharply, "and take Glasco—"

Clem Barnes' startled eyes were wide and unbelieving, but the paralyzing grip of steel fingers digging into his arm and the compelling fire in Rockwell's piercing black eyes shocked him into action. Three long strides carried him to the score table where he reported for Peters. Then he was back in the huddle between Rockwell and Chip.

The tumult of exultation which had subsided during the time-out now arose again, only this time it was a swelling babble of surprise out of which came angry shouts and threats.

In front of the home bench, Coach Russ Whitcomb was talking earnestly to his players. One boy shook his head and sat down on the bench and another followed. A cheer went up, then, evidently for those two boys who refused to play against a colored boy. But when Whitcomb beckoned, two other players arose from the bench and came forward.

The referee's whistle shrilled, but when the Big Reds and Clem Barnes started out on the floor you would have thought a giant bomb had exploded in the building. The bedlam of yells and catcalls were too much for a sensitive youngster like Clem Barnes to take. He turned and walked back to the bench. Rockwell blocked him at the edge of the court and Barnes stopped there. His stricken eyes lifted to Rockwell's face. And his voice was trembling a little as he whispered the words, but soft as they were, Rockwell heard them—heard them as clear as a bell.

"I don't want to play against them if they don't want to play against me, Coach."

Then Clem Barnes sank down on the bench and his head dropped forward and he sat there and he never heard a thing.

The shouting and the yelling died down a bit, then, and almost ceased entirely a second later, when the captain of Southern High School's basketball team walked deliberately over to the Valley Falls bench and reached down and grasped Clem Barnes by the hand. And Clem Barnes never remembered being led out on that floor, nor playing out the remainder of that game.

When the game was over, the first Negro boy ever to play against a white boy in the town of Southern never heard the deafening cheers which went up from the packed stands. And he never knew that many of those cheers were for him.

When that great crowd of hoop crazy fans filed soberly out of that building a few minutes later, they knew that Southern had upset the state champions. They knew that, for some reason, the victory hadn't been as thrilling as they had expected. Some knew that the score had been 41 to 35. And some knew that Valley Falls had scored eleven points in the last few minutes while Southern was scoring three. Some even grudgingly admitted that the Negro boy was a good basketball player.

But some were bitter and some were angry and some were ashamed. A few were proud, like the middle-aged man and his wife who made their way quietly toward the modest little home down near the river where a little name plate bearing the name of Berrien was tacked to the gatepost by the walk. And these two and many others could still see Southern's gallant young captain leading the Negro boy from Valley Falls out on to the floor.

And most of those who walked out into the clean, cool night air after that great Southern victory somehow felt pride in the realization that the captain of the kids who represented their high school and their town was a courageous, bighearted boy who wasn't afraid to be a man.

CHAPTER 14

FIRE DEPARTMENT BASKETBALL

George Hankins, effusive, efficient, gracious, and clever manager of the Southern Hotel was surprised when the Valley Falls High School basketball team checked out that same night right after their squad supper. He was relieved, he had to admit to himself, but he professed to be extremely sorry when he said good-bye to Rogers and Chet Stewart.

"Tell the coach not to forget us the next time he's in Southern. And better luck next time."

All the Big Reds were glad to get out of that town. Glad to be on their way home. They had all expressed that desire when Rockwell said they could wander around, if they wanted to, so long as they checked in at midnight. But they didn't want to and they said so. They wanted to go home! Rockwell and Rogers debated the matter briefly and agreed that it was a good idea.

It was only ten thirty when the red-and-white bus pulled away from the Southern Hotel and with good luck they would be home in two and a half hours. The driver clicked off the lights and the only conversation was the muffled talk of some of the JV's who hadn't understood and hadn't caught the significance of the crowd's reaction to Clem Barnes.

Most of the boys slouched down in their seats and tried to sleep. But Chip Hilton, Clem Barnes, Soapy Smith, Biggie Cohen, and Speed Morris were wide awake. They were thinking about many things.

Chip was thinking of his mother and how she must have felt when she heard the score. Then he began thinking of the wide rift in the feelings and in the play of the Big Reds. Speed and Red and even Soapy had gone completely overboard with the long one-handers and with the kind of basketball the Independents were playing. Then Chip's thoughts swung around to the stranger, to T. A. K. Baxter. Rockwell had called the university just as he said he would and they had said, "Yes, sure, Rock, we had a Baxter here. Played one year of varsity basketball, I think. But there was a Baxter here—"

Clem Barnes was still in a fog. It had been a nightmare. He was disconsolate that the team had lost, though he knew he had done his level best.

Biggie Cohen was getting fed up with Buzz Todd and Red Schwartz and Speed Morris. He knew the team was being wrecked because of the one-hand shooting of these three fellows who had been and were yet, he hoped, his friends. The team play was shot and Chip wasn't getting the ball and Biggie didn't know what to do about it. He was worried most, though, about the restraint which was plainly noticeable in the friendship of Chip, Speed, Red, and Buzz.

Rockwell sat in a front seat next to Rogers and he hadn't spoken a word since he had taken his seat. He was going back through the years to the time when he had first realized the enormity of this racial question. There hadn't been much progress, he decided. For a long time he had known that Pop Brown always had "friends" to stay with when he traveled with the team. But Pop's position was a little different from that of Clem Barnes. Clem was on the team and the team played and stuck together.

Late that night it began to snow and, when Mary Hilton called Chip the next morning, it was ankle-deep. Chip hustled outside and began shoveling a path to the sidewalk. He was glad to have something to do so he wouldn't have to talk about the game. But he couldn't entirely escape his mother's questions at the breakfast table. Mary Hilton sensed Chip's despondency and she couldn't resist trying to help him.

"What's happening to the team, Chip?"

Chip took a sip of milk and then told his mother all about the incident at Southern and about the team and how it wasn't a team at all now. He was almost bitter as he talked, choosing his words carefully and trying to be fair. It was as though he was trying to figure it all out for himself as he spoke.

"Bill Berrien was great, Mother. That crowd was as close to a mob, I guess, as there ever was. Berrien just took hold of Clem's hand and led him out on the floor and then he and the Southern boys lined up and we lined up and the game went on—

"And, Mother," Chip said reflectively, "Berrien played against Barnes. He'd been playing against me, you know, and he shifted over against Clem for the rest of the game and when it was over he shook hands with Clem and slapped him on the back and walked clear over to our bench with him."

Mrs. Hilton knew that wasn't all that was worrying her son, so she waited patiently for him to continue.

"Mother," Chip said anxiously, "have you noticed any difference in Speed and Red and Soapy, lately? Gee, when the season first started we worked hard and we worked as a team. Now, it's each fellow for himself, or so it seems."

Chip then told his mother about Buzz Todd and the way he had been playing and what he had to say about Chip's high scoring. He told her about the team's obsession for long one-handers, but he was careful to leave Baxter out of it in every way.

"Buzz said I was sore because I wasn't making all the points and now I wish I hadn't said anything to him. I'm sure not going to say anything to anyone else."

Mary Hilton could think of no way to help her son in his predicament, so she probably did the best thing possible. She smiled encouragingly and patted him on the shoulder. They walked to work together, Indian file, with Chip leading the way through the freshly fallen snow. At the telephone office Chip kissed his mother lightly on the cheek and trudged on down Main Street to the Sugar Bowl. He had the first hour of that day to himself and he was glad because he was in no mood to explain to Petey or to John Schroeder what had happened.

Midway in the morning Petey came barging back into the storeroom with Soapy right behind him.

"Hey, Chip," he said excitedly, "look at what Kennedy says in today's *Times*. Here, read it!"

Chip reluctantly read the column while Petey and Soapy hung over his shoulder.

TIMES AND SPORTS
By Joe Kennedy

The Big Reds' hopes for the successful defense of their state title took another nose dive last night at Southern when the boys from the big river section handed the locals their second straight setback by a score of 41 to 35.

The score is misleading . . . The game was anything but close . . . Valley Falls was completely subdued as early as the end of the first quarter when they trailed 14 to 3. . . . During the second period the Southerners took the locals completely apart and led at the half 23 to 9.

Things got worse in the third quarter and at the end of the period Southern led, 34 to 18. Coach Russ Whitcomb ordered his boys to ease up in the fourth quarter and that condescension enabled the state champions to save a little face in what might easily have been a rout.

Clem Barnes played in the final minutes of the game and, according to reports received by this reporter, looked just as good in a varsity uniform as he has looked with the Little Reds.

What has happened to Chip Hilton's shooting eye? . . . Hilton's early scoring spurt is holding his game average to 19.3 per game . . . But in the last four games Hilton has scored 14 . . . 12 . . . 9 . . . and 12 points, respectively . . . High-scoring records are not broken with totals like those.

The Independents continued on their merry way to the establishment of all-time individual and team scoring records in this fair village if not in the state.

And that brings to mind a thought for local civic and service clubs who have been groping around for a means of raising money for the Damon Runyon Cancer Fund . . . So . . . Why not stage a game at the high school between the Big Reds and the Independents?

Local interest in the game would be tremendous. . . . Speculation has already been rife and arguments pro and con advanced concerning the ability of the Big Reds to cope with the hard-pressing and high-scoring attack used by Coach T. A. K. Baxter's hard-driving Independents.

Just for the record, let's check the Independents' score book . . . In seven games they have scored exactly 648 points for an average of 92 points per game . . . *Ninety-two points per game.*

On the other side of the ledger the Big Reds have scored

428 points in ten games for a game average of 42.8.

What do you think of the idea, fans? . . . The Big Reds play Parkton next Friday night, January 17, and Weston away on Wednesday the 22 . . . The Independents play on the 15 and the 20 . . . WHY NOT STAGE THE GAME ON SATURDAY . . . JANUARY 25 . . . FOR THE DAMON RUNYON CANCER FUND?

Soapy grabbed the paper and wadded it into a ball. Then he threw it up at the ceiling. "Can you imagine that guy," he said sarcastically, "just because we lose a game— Hah!"

"What about the Independents, Chip?" Petey asked curiously. "You guys afraid of them? You think Rock would play them?"

Soapy turned as though he had been stung by a hornet and nearly jabbed a finger through Petey's throat. "Afraid of them?" Soapy yelled incredulously. "Afraid of them?" he repeated. "Are you losin' your mind? Why, we'd kill 'em! Kill 'em, I tell you, kill 'em piece by piece!"

"Yeah," Petey said, shaking a skinny forefinger in Soapy's face. "Yeah? Why, you guys couldn't carry their shoes! You ain't got nobody on the whole team 'cept Chip, here, who can throw the ball in the ocean. Who's gonna score for you? Huh? And who's gonna stop them one-handers Baxter taught 'em? Kill 'em! Huh! Why they'll beat you fifty points! Heck, looky here! Look at what Pete Williams says here in the *Post!* Heck, he says the same thing! Listen!"

" 'Aside from the Cancer Fund benefits, the contest will give local hoop enthusiasts an opportunity to compare the slam-bang, fire department brand of basketball coached by T. A. K. Baxter, with the more conservative style favored by Rockwell. The Independents undoubtedly carry too many guns for the kids but, since the cause is worth while and the contest would be purely an exhibition, it seems a swell idea. This reporter is all for it and all for the Cancer Fund!' "

Petey looked at Soapy triumphantly. "Well," he said complacently, "what do you think about that?"

Soapy was on the defensive now, but he wasn't at a loss for words. "Aw, what do those two crackpots know about basketball!" he said aggressively. "Why, neither one of 'em ever played anything but horseshoes."

That hurt Petey. Everyone in town knew he was the best horseshoe pitcher around. "And what's the matter with horseshoes?" he demanded. "Takes skill, don't it? Takes a good eye to make a ringer, don't it?' "

Soapy was disgusted. "Skill? Good eye? Ringer? Hah! Let me out of here before I hang a ringer on your eye."

The argument between Petey and Soapy saved Chip further embarrassment. But Petey and Soapy had company. It seemed that every person in town had got into it. And they took sides.

Doc Jones thought the Independents were terrific. "They'll beat the kids thirty points!"

John Schroeder stuck with Rockwell and with the Big Reds. "The kids play a sounder game. They have a better defense! The Independents have been playing push-overs!"

CHAPTER 15

MR. BAXTER RETURNS

WHILE Rockwell was thinking about last year's state champions and what he could do to pull them together again, his players were thinking about the Independents and what they were going to do about them on Saturday, January 25. Somewhat against his will the coach had yielded to the public clamor and arranged a game with the town team to be played for charity. Soapy was his old self once again and led the verbal assault on the town team.

"Wait till we get at 'em. Wish we were playin' 'em *this* Saturday. We'll kill 'em!"

"Don't forget we've got two games before the twenty-fifth," Chip reminded him, "and they're both tough!"

"We'll start rolling now," Biggie said confidently.

Speed Morris was nodding his head grimly. "Maybe someone else can net one-handers," he said dryly. "If Chip doesn't outscore Joe Kelly, I'll stop playing basketball—" He stopped abruptly and looked around at the circle of faces. Speed was grinning as he continued, "The way I've been playing, it looks as though I've stopped already."

Rockwell might have utilized a bit of psychology with

respect to the coming game with the Independents to bring his team together again if he could have heard this conversation. But he was faraway and, in addition, perhaps did not realize what a deep impression the stranger's long showboat one-handers had made upon Buzz Todd, Speed Morris, Red Schwartz, and Soapy Smith.

So all week he kept shifting his line-up and, as the novelty of the coming game with the Independents wore off, the players began to drift apart again.

When Chip got home from practice Thursday evening, he was feeling especially glum. The practice had been exceptionally bad that night. Rockwell had again divided the squad and that seemed to create bad humor on the part of everyone.

Chip opened the street door and met his mother in the hall carrying the vacuum cleaner. "Hey, where you going with that?" he demanded, kissing her and gently taking the machine out of her hand.

Mrs. Hilton smiled. "Why, I was going upstairs to vacuum Mr. Baxter's room. He'll be home tomorrow. At least he said he'd be back on Friday."

Chip carried the vacuum up the steps and into the bedroom occupied by Baxter. The room had that stale tobacco odor which identifies a chain smoker and which permeates a room when the windows have been tightly closed for a period of time. Chip sniffed and, without thinking, opened the window. A gust of wind flooded the room and sent all the papers lying on the desk by the window whirling about the room and to the floor.

Chip hastily closed the window and helped his mother pick up the papers. They were concerned with formulas and pottery and were evidently being prepared for Mr. Baxter's book. Chip could tell that from the brief glance he gave them, but the thing that caused both mother and son to stop and stare was the newspaper picture of T. A. K. Baxter. It headed a newspaper article which said it was one of a series that the distinguished chemist, T. A. K. Baxter, was writing concerning the history and development of ceramic engineering in the colleges and universities of the United States.

Chip and his mother peered at the clipping intently.

"Why, it doesn't even look like him," Chip said slowly.

Mrs. Hilton held the paper up to the light of the window and shook her head. "No, it doesn't," she agreed.

They both looked for the date and then Mrs. Hilton expressed the thought which each was thinking. "But this picture was taken ten years ago and Mr. Baxter wasn't wearing a mustache, then. The eyes seem the same, though, and he appears a lot heavier in the picture."

Chip studied the eyes but, so far as he could see, there was no real resemblance. Nothing more was said, but that article had set Chip thinking again. Something about this man just didn't click. Chip wished he could put his finger on what it was.

All through dinner Chip couldn't get his mind away from Baxter. He finished his dinner and glanced at the clock. He had a few minutes left before it was time to leave for the Sugar Bowl and his steps led him down into the cellar and toward Big Chip Hilton's little laboratory. Ever since reading the article and studying Baxter's picture, Chip had been thinking about pottery.

He unlocked the door, clicked on the light, and picked up one of the pieces of his father's pottery. The pieces of ware were of the same design and shape and Chip ran his fingers lightly over each of the five. The last one was a little further back on the table and as soon as Chip touched it he noticed the difference. The finish was irregular and the weight did not seem the same. He wondered why he had never noticed that before. But he replaced it and hurried off to the Sugar Bowl without thinking much more about it.

The East-West Limited arrived in Valley Falls right on time at two twenty-seven and stopped long enough to let T. A. K. Baxter and two or three other persons alight. Then it slid silently away.

Baxter was in excellent spirits and greeted two or three persons he recognized on his way to the taxi stand. He held the traveling bag he carried with a tight grip, refusing the driver's offer of aid. And when he lifted the bag carefully to the seat beside him he kept a hand glued to the handle. The taxi carried him straight up Main Street, past the Sugar Bowl and up the little hill and then to the right for three blocks to the house with the white picket fence.

Baxter smiled grimly as he paid the driver and he grasped the thin little roll of bills. He'd have to move along fast now. Start thinking about his approach to J. P. Ohlsen. As he placed the bag on the front porch and fumbled in his pocket for the key to the door, there was a pleased expression on his face. That little handbag held the last stone, or stones, if you wanted to be technical, to the path which should lead T. A. K. Baxter to financial security.

There was no one home and he hurried upstairs to his room and hastily unpacked the five little pieces of ware. From a distance they were identical with the five pieces which reposed on the table in the basement. All except one. That one was an original and must be put in the place of the crude duplicate he had made and which was, even now, he fervently hoped, resting safely on the table beside the four originals in the cellar.

A little later Baxter, first making sure Mrs. Browning

was not in sight, hurried down to the cellar to substitute the original piece of ware for the poor imitation he had placed far back on the table. His heart jumped when he saw that the pieces had been moved, and he examined them carefully before he hurried back upstairs to his room. What if the kid had discovered the substitution? The pieces had been moved. That could mean trouble. He'd have to be careful. He couldn't afford to have anything go wrong now. Well, he could read women like Mary Hilton and kids like Chip Hilton like a book. He'd be able to tell by their actions when they came home.

The three hours which followed were long and anxious ones for T. A. K. Baxter. This scheme had been so cleverly worked out and was moving along so beautifully that it would be a shame for some little thing to upset the applecart now.

Baxter made sure to be in the living room when Mary Hilton came hurrying home. The warmth in her greeting reassured him. Now he knew it was the kid he'd have to worry about.

Chip had gone directly to the Sugar Bowl after school and had been kept busy until six o'clock. Then he hurried home to have a light supper before going to school for the game with Parkton. He hoped Baxter had not yet arrived home. When he found him chatting with Mrs. Hilton in the living room, the boy's gray eyes clouded with disappointment.

Baxter was enthusiastic in his greeting, but his sharp eyes were alert and observing as he studied Chip's face when they gripped hands. He breathed a little sigh of relief and satisfaction when he noted no apparent change in Chip's manner. The kid had never been too friendly, but there was no new restraint in his greeting. Baxter felt sure everything was all right.

CHAPTER 16

VARSITY SHAKE-UP

It was exactly seven thirty Friday night when Rockwell opened the door to the Big Reds' dressing room, and the boys didn't have to look up to know who it was.

Rockwell cleared his throat and waited until every boy gave him his attention. Then he began talking about Parkton.

"They're big and they fight and they work hard off the boards. They use a switch defense. That means that they trade opponents every time an opponent crosses in front of them. They look for interceptions all the time. They play "dummy" most of the time until they catch you napping and making a sloppy, careless pass and then they make a dart for the ball and for the interception.

"When they get the ball they break down the floor for the little gift you were kind enough to make— The two points you gave away. The second time that happens to one of you tonight, you just start walking and walk right over to the bench and sit down beside me.

"Now as an offense against their switch defense, we'll change direction when we're in the backcourt and cut right down the middle. Instead of crossing in a weave

136

or a roll, we'll start as if we're going to do that and then we'll change direction and cut through toward the basket. Maybe one of you can drag both of the men who are getting ready to switch with you and then the other man will be free for an easy 'front-of-the-basket' shot.

"On the defense we'll play a straight man-to-man defense with no switching. Each one of you will be responsible for your own man."

Every person in that room waited for Rockwell to name the usual starters. That would be Browning, Morris, Hilton, Todd, and Schwartz. But there were several players there who waited with a thumping heart, hoping that this would be the night that Rock would call his name.

"Browning at center, Hilton and Schwartz up front—"

Yep . . . It was the same old line-up.

"Morris and Barnes at the guards! Let's go!"

They all sprang to their feet and rushed to the rubbing table to join hands with Rockwell in the usual pre-game team grip. Then they followed Chip Hilton out the door and up the hall and out onto the court. As each boy passed through the door, Rockwell thumped him on the back and just as he stepped down to the hall level, Pop Brown added his, "Let's go!"

After Pop Brown's "Let's go," each boy trotted after Chip and they were all thinking the same thing: Rock had benched Buzz Todd for Clem Barnes.

Chip was thinking that Buzz would be sore at him. Maybe think he had said something to Rock about their differences with respect to shooting and scoring.

Speed Morris was thinking that Rock had a lot of nerve to put Barnes in Todd's place. Why, Buzz was a veteran and one of the best shots in the state. . . . Well, with two hands. And the way he was improving with the long one-handers he'd soon be the best in the state with that shot too.

Buzz Todd was bitter and was thinking just what Chip Hilton had been afraid he'd think.

Taps Browning wasn't thinking much about it. He didn't care who Rockwell put on the team just so he left Chip Hilton on it. And Taps Browning.

Red Schwartz was a little glad. But he wished it had been Soapy instead of Barnes to take Todd's place. He didn't go for this and Speed wouldn't either. What in the world was Chip thinking about when he started pitching horseshoes for Clem Barnes?

Soapy Smith was thinking that maybe it wasn't a bad idea to get someone in there in Todd's place. Buzz had been throwing the ball away with too many bad shots. A guy could spot bad shooting better when he was sitting on the bench. He ought to know. He'd been sitting plenty so far. Maybe Rock would give him a chance if Barnes fell down.

Clem Barnes was wishing this hadn't happened. He didn't want to play this bad. Didn't want to take any varsity player's place. He wasn't good enough and most of the fellows didn't want to play with him . . . excepting Chip and Taps and Teddy and Fred and maybe Soapy Smith.

Parkton was tough. Chip and all the other Big Reds knew that just as soon as they got the ball and tried to penetrate the switch defense. Taps beat the Parkton center to the jump and Chip came in high on the signal and took the ball. Then he passed to Speed and pivoted toward the right corner so the middle of the court would be open. That would make it easy for Speed and Barnes and Red to change direction and cut down the middle according to Rockwell's instructions. But Speed didn't pass the ball to Schwartz or Barnes, change direction, and then cut down the middle of the court. He continued on with the ball, dribbling for all he was worth. And he ran into a stone wall of closing-in or floating Parkton players who gummed up the middle and took the ball away from him.

The Parkton switch defense was a lot like a zone when a fellow tried to drive through with the ball. It closed up tight. Some coaches call this method of "ganging-up" on the man with the ball, "sagging" or "floating." Rockwell maintained it was really a zone defense and that anyone who claimed that he used a pure man-to-man or a switch defense and combined floating in it was inconsistent. But no matter what you called Parkton's defense, it was effective. The fact that he had lost the ball seemed to infuriate Speed and he bullheadedly tried it again and again.

Rockwell surprised every member of the squad, then, because, for the first time in three years, Speed Morris came out of a game in the first five minutes of play.

Morris was burning up when Teddy Rice came trotting out on the floor in his place. But Speed was a good sport at heart and though he tried to mask his feelings it was evident to all that he was angry and hurt.

The customary Big Reds procedure was for any player who left the floor to come directly to the bench and sit down beside Rockwell in the place which had just been vacated by the boy reporting in his place. Morris never gave it a thought. He had rarely left a game at all in the three years he had played. Now he was angry because he hadn't been able to break through the switch defense and a little ashamed of his bullheaded persistence. So it was not strange that he forgot all about sitting down on the bench beside his coach.

Rockwell was a considerate man. He made it a per-

sonal rule to pat the outcoming boy on the shoulder and
to give him a smile and an "Okay, boy," but he never
added to that greeting until the game was on again and
the attention of the spectators directed to the contest.
Then he would talk to the boy, point out his mistakes or
give him instructions with respect to a change in his
personal play or outline a revised team offense or defense.

When Speed came off the court, Rockwell expected
him to come directly to the vacant place on the bench.
But the angry guard hurried to the extreme end of the
bench, looking neither to the right nor to the left.
Rockwell half rose, apparently to call Speed, but then
he seemed to change his mind and, instead, motioned
to Soapy Smith to sit beside him. So it was Soapy who
got the instructions Rockwell had planned to give
Speed Morris. Rockwell spoke in a low voice to Soapy,
explaining why he had sent Teddy Rice in to take the
veteran guard's place.

"You can't dribble through that kind of defense,
Soapy. You've got to use a give-and-go type of offense
from the backcourt, unless you pass the ball forward
to a side-post man and then cut down the middle for a
return pass. Keep in mind that the strength of the switch
defense is based upon clogging up the center of the
court in front of the basket. That's why we've got Chip
and Taps playing out of the base-line corners. Get it?
Okay. Now relax and watch— You'll probably be in
there in a couple minutes!"

Soapy wasn't in there in a couple of minutes and
neither was Speed Morris. Teddy Rice was teaming up
beautifully with Clem Barnes in give-and-go plays
which Chet Stewart had drilled into them day after
day. And the plays and Teddy and Clem were all click-
ing. First, Teddy would pass to Clem and reverse direc-

tion to receive the return pass and score. Then it would be Barnes who would work the play. It did not take long for the Big Reds' rooters to get behind the two kids.

"Look at those kids go!"

"Beats everything *I* ever saw!"

Up in the center of the stands, directly opposite the ten-second line which split the middle of the court, big, happy-go-lucky Jim Rice turned to Mrs. Rice and nearly submerged her with the big, wide smile which had been one of the important factors in building up his hardware business to the point where it was the best store of its kind in the state. Mrs. Rice was smiling, too, but she kept her eyes fixed on the kid who had taken Morris' place. And she nodded her head when Jim Rice said that the colored boy was working well with Teddy, and that they made a good combination, all right, and that Rockwell was really something the way he could put his finger on the right combination.

At the half Parkton led, 22 to 17, but the respectability of the score was due to the almost singlehanded scoring efforts of Teddy Rice and Clem Barnes. The Valley Falls scorebook, the official book because it was the home team's, had four X's behind Clem Barnes' name in the field-goal column and there were two X's in the field-goal column and one X in the free-throw column on the line beside Teddy Rice's name. Yes, those two kids had made thirteen of Valley Fall's seventeen points!

When the second half began, everyone noticed that Rockwell had made no change in the line-up with which the first half had ended. Henry Rockwell believed in keeping a winning combination intact as long as possible. But after three minutes of second-half play, it was evident, even to Mrs. Rice, that something was wrong. The give-and-go plays of the former JV captain and Clem Barnes were no longer effective. In fact, the two "upped" JV players had lost the ball the first three times they tried the plays which had worked so well toward the end of the first half and Parkton was now out in front, 28 to 17.

Rockwell stood up and Chip immediately called time and the Big Reds followed him over to huddle around Rockwell in front of the bench.

"Won't do, boys," Rockwell said, shaking his head. "We've got to change our attack. They're not switching now. Just standing there in the keyhole in front of the basket and picking off the backcourt passes we're throwing down the middle."

He turned and looked down at the end of the bench where Morris and Buzz Todd were sitting side by side. He eyed them darkly a moment and then beckoned to Soapy Smith and Lefty Peters. They joined the huddle and Rockwell patted Clem Barnes and Teddy Rice on the shoulder and told them to sit down. "Nice work, kids." Then he turned back to the huddle.

"Pay attention now," he barked. "Chip, you work right under the basket as you did year before last. Taps, you go to the left corner, and Schwartz—you take the right corner. We'll play close to the base line. Maybe that'll keep them from floating. Soapy, you and Lefty will try to work the ball to the corners, either corner. And from the corners we'll try to get the ball to Chip under the basket. If we can't get it in to Chip, the opposite corner man will cut across and in front of Chip and the player in the corner with the ball will feed the ball to this cutter. Get it? Clear? No? Well, listen—

"We'll suppose Red has the ball in the right corner and can't get the ball to Chip. Taps, you cut around in front of Chip and toward the ball and then Schwartz will try to hit you coming toward the basket. Clear? Good!

"Now, suppose Red can't pass to Chip under the basket and he can't get the ball to Taps cutting across— Just as soon as Taps passes you, Chip, you back up to the free-throw line. Then, Red, you feed Chip the ball with a high, hard pass. And, Chip, I want you to shoot every time you get the ball no matter where that happens to be—under the basket or out on the free-throw line! That's an order! Now—"

The timekeeper's buzzer sounded just then and Rockwell gestured impatiently toward the scorer's table. Then he pushed Chip toward the referee standing with the ball just outside their huddle. "Tell him we want another time-out, Chip. Two in a row!"

Chip called the second consecutive time-out and, as soon as he rejoined the huddle, Rockwell continued.

"Now, Chip and Taps and Schwartz—I want you three boys to follow-in every shot and keep bouncing that ball back up on that board just as though you were playing volleyball! Get it? Okay."

Rockwell turned to Soapy Smith and jabbed a hard forefinger in that worthy's chest. "You," he said harshly, "you used to have a good two-hand set shot. Well, every time your guard drops back to stop the under-basket stuff I want you to fire away at that basket. Red or Taps or Chip will get the ball to you. But no one-handers! Understand? Okay! Let's go in there and do it and win this game! Report, Soapy! You, too, Lefty!"

For the next five minutes it looked as though Rockwell's revised attack might do the trick. Chip scored every point the Big Reds made in the next five minutes. Six straight goals in ten shots, and, at the end of the third quarter, the score was: Parkton 34, Valley Falls 29.

When play was resumed in the fourth quarter, it was evident to every Valley Falls basketball fan that Parkton was concentrating on stopping Chip Hilton. They double-teamed him, blocked him away from the basket, fouled him, and did everything but tie him with a rope. Those tactics cut down on his scoring effectiveness, all right, but Chip passed-off time and again to Schwartz and Soapy when two Parkton players shifted to stop his shots. But Red was off and Soapy couldn't seem to come even close with his two-hand sets.

At that, Chip got eight points, one field goal and six free throws. But the rest of the Big Reds could only score five points and that wasn't quite enough. Parkton lasted it out to hand Valley Falls' sharpshooters their third straight defeat and win 43 to 42.

Once again, the group of boys who piled into Speed's jalopy were ill at ease and aware of that new strangeness which seemed to make conversation difficult. Speed was hurt and quiet and Chip didn't know what to say. Irrepressible Soapy, however, couldn't be stilled and reproached Speed for not sitting down beside Rockwell when he came out of the game.

"But, Soapy," Speed remonstrated, "I forgot all about it! It never entered my mind!"

"That's easy to understand," Chip said quickly. "Heck, Speed's always played about every minute of every game. Anyone could make that mistake."

"Yeah, sure," Biggie Cohen drawled, "but we'd have won that game if Speed hadn't overlooked the fact that Rock might have desired to convey a little information to him. And I don't think Rock felt very good about the way Buzz was sulking."

Speed nodded his head in self-reproach. "Yes," he said, "I *would* sit down there beside Buzz. Rock probably thinks I was sulking, too!"

CHAPTER 17

BIG REDS' TAIL SPIN

SUNDAY had always been a day of rest in the Hilton home and Chip looked forward to it all week. The everyday grind of school, practice, work, and study took a lot out of him. More important, Sunday was the only day he could enjoy a long visit with his mother. It was an important day for Mrs. Hilton, too. The weekdays were long days for her, considering she had to cook, clean, sew, mend and wash clothes, and still maintain her rigorous job as supervisor of the telephone exchange. So it was no wonder that the Hiltons looked forward eagerly to their Sundays at home.

Before the arrival of Baxter, the Sunday timetable called for late sleeping, late breakfast, leisurely perusal of the *Post* and the *Times,* church always, two o'clock dinner, the assembly of the members of the Hilton A. C. at any time but always by three o'clock. Refreshments at five and then more gabfest by the members in which Mrs. Hilton often joined, a cold snack at seven, and then schoolbooks for Chip and reading for Mrs. Hilton until early bedtime.

Taps Browning had a part in most of the Sunday program even to crawling into the extra bed in Chip's room more often than he crawled into his own next door. Soapy Smith was taken for granted. He was just as likely to turn up at eight o'clock in the morning as seven at night. But regular as a clock he always made his appearance in time for two-o'clock dinner and reluctantly permitted himself to be escorted to the table. As Soapy himself said, he was an epicure.

The Sunday program had been customary for years and enjoyed by all concerned until T. A. K. Baxter had maneuvered himself into the middle of things in the Hilton household. Then, little by little, the routine had changed. Taps began to stay home more often, Soapy didn't show up quite so early nor stay so long, and the other members of the crowd began to appear less frequently. Chip didn't like this new scheme of things, but Mary Hilton, charmed by Baxter's glib stories of Big Chip Hilton, didn't even notice the change.

When Chip came down the stairs the Sunday morning following the Parkton game, his mother and Baxter were in the living room reading the papers. Baxter greeted Chip cordially and held out the *Times*.

"Says here you're back in stride again," he said. "Saw the game myself, and I thought you were splendid. Here, read the story."

Mrs. Hilton interrupted. "Yes, Chip, and read the story on the front page, too. We're going to lose Mr. Baxter very soon. Sorry to say. He's going to England!"

The glance Chip turned toward Baxter was questioning, but it was hopeful, too. Baxter read the boy's glance correctly and his mouth twitched with a little smile.

"Yes," he said, stroking the small, graying mustache he affected, "I'm afraid I'll have to leave your beautiful little town, Chip, in a week or so. Probably the week following our game."

He smiled again and added, "People will probably run me out of town after you high school fellows give my Independents a shellacking!"

Mrs. Hilton pointed to the front page of the paper she held. "It says here in the *Post* that Mr. Baxter is being sent to England by the Gately Pottery Company to make arrangements for the purchase of five million dollars worth of English clay. *Five million dollars worth!*"

"That's right," Baxter said modestly, "and then I'm going to spend a couple of months on the Continent and rest up. Writing a book isn't as easy as a lot of people think. Especially if it's concerned with a technical subject."

"Is the book nearly finished?" Mary Hilton asked.

Baxter assured her that it was and then went into a long discourse concerning his new discoveries in the field of ceramics and how he hoped to use them to revolutionize American methods of producing pottery of all kinds.

Chip welcomed this opportunity to escape to the cellar, taking the paper with him. He unlocked the door and sat down to read what Joe Kennedy had to say about the game.

TIMES AND SPORTS

By Joe Kennedy

Valley Falls' state champs lost their third straight last night. . . . Rockwell's veterans, with the exception of Chip Hilton, seem to be skidding fast. . . . The return of Hilton's shooting eye was the only redeeming feature of a dull contest.

Is Buzz Todd definitely shelved? . . . And are reports that he turned in his uniform last night authentic? . . .

Rockwell didn't use Todd at all last night . . . What is wrong with Speed Morris? . . . He played only the first few minutes of the contest.

What has happened to the scoring of Schwartz, Browning, and Morris? . . . Seems to this observer that . . . as Chip Hilton goes . . . so go the Big Reds . . . When he doesn't score the game isn't even close. . . . Parkton gave Hilton the works last night, but he hit for 20 points.

Teddy Rice, former JV captain, played a good second quarter . . . So did his JV teammate, Clem Barnes. . . . These youngsters show plenty of promise, but still need "big time" experience.

The Big Reds–Independents game scheduled for Saturday, January 25, is sold out . . . Damon Runyon Cancer Fund benefits . . . The high school's five-thousand-seat capacity could be doubled and would still be inadequate to handle the fans who want to see the game.

Independents are favored . . . More experience . . . Bigger . . . Five scorers . . . Kelly, Dobson, Steup, Spotts, and Moore are all expert marksmen . . . They can really throw that little old pill through the ring.

The intracity contest may mark the last appearance of T. A. K. Baxter as coach of the Independents . . . He leaves for England shortly to purchase some English clay for a big domestic concern . . . Baxter's chemical discoveries may revolutionize American pottery methods.

Hope you have your ticket for the Cancer Fund game . . . See you there.

Chip tossed the paper on the table and breathed a sigh of relief. So Baxter was leaving. Couldn't be soon enough for him.

He picked up one of the five little pieces of pottery and his thoughts went back to the rough piece. He examined each one carefully and was surprised to find that they were almost identical and the rough piece seemed to have disappeared. Maybe he had imagined

it! No, it had been real enough. . . . He examined each
of the pieces again. No, they were all alike. Each was
as smooth and perfect in balance and weight as the
others. He couldn't have dreamed it!

While Chip was at home and down in the cellar,
Biggie Cohen was at the Sugar Bowl talking to Soapy
Smith. Biggie didn't like the way things had been going
with the team and he didn't like the way things were
going with Soapy and Speed and Buzz and Red and
Chip Hilton. And he had decided to do something
about it.

Soapy Smith was first on Biggie's list and he was glad
to find the clown alone in the Sugar Bowl. Biggie lowered himself gingerly to a seat on one of the table chairs
and shook a massive finger toward Soapy who was leaning forward with his elbows on the top of the fountain.

"Look, my friend," Biggie began, "you and I have to
have a little understanding. *You* are one of the chief
reasons this ball club of ours is going on the rocks!"

Soapy's eyes opened wide with surprise and he
straightened up with amazement written all over his
face. "Me? Well how do you like that? Me?"

"Yes, *you!* You're one of the chief offenders. And
Speed's another, and Buzz is another and Red's another—"

Soapy's mouth opened wide and the lower lip
dropped in astonishment. "You out of your mind?" he
managed.

Then Biggie let him have it. No, he wasn't out of his
mind! But Soapy Smith was! Soapy Smith and Speed
Morris and Buzz Todd and Red Schwartz.

The team had been swell until everyone began to go
shot crazy! It was no longer a team—it was a bunch of
heavers. And all because a bunch of pickup, run-down,
group of has-beens known as the Valley Falls Inde-

pendents were beating a few one-horse, country-store basketball teams—

Yes, and because Soapy and the rest of them had fallen for a vaudeville exhibitionist who had played basketball before the Civil War and who had mesmerized just about every person in town because he could shoot a basketball with one hand—

So the best team in the state begins to look like Public School Six and Rock has to bring up a couple of kids from the kindergarten to bolster an outfit which should beat any high school team in the country—

There was more and it was backed up by two hundred and thirty pounds of fighting spirit and Soapy Smith took it and liked it. After Biggie Cohen stalked out of the Sugar Bowl on the prowl for Speed Morris, Buzz Todd, and Red Schwartz, a redheaded high school soda jerk, who had never been very serious about anything except eating and athletics, stood there so long and so quietly that Petey Jackson figured he was sick.

But Soapy wasn't sick. He was thinking that every player on the team with the exception of Chip had been a fool. Chip had tried to reason with the fellows and had sacrificed his own scoring to prove to them that he didn't want to hog the headlines as Buzz Todd had claimed.

Soapy was sorry about Buzz Todd. Buzz was a pretty good guy, but he was undependable and always seemed to be in trouble. Last year, right in the stretch when every player was needed, Rockwell had been forced to drop him from the squad for breaking training.

Soapy banged a fist so hard on the fountain that it hurt. He was starting "as of now" to do his part to get the team back in the groove and to patch up the hard feelings which were gripping certain persons he knew. Biggie Cohen had the right dope.

Biggie didn't do quite so well with Buzz Todd. Buzz was adamant. No, he was through and that was that! He'd already turned in his suit and he wasn't going back even if Rockwell got down on his knees!

"But you're the one that quit!" Biggie reminded him. "Rock didn't tell you to turn in your suit!"

"Yeah, but he benched me, didn't he? Benched me for a JV, didn't he? Made me look like two cents, didn't he?"

Biggie talked to Buzz Todd for over an hour, trying to explain that Rockwell was probably right in benching him because he hadn't been hitting with his wild, long one-handers and, besides, he was undoubtedly the best two-hand set shot in the state and Rock had depended upon him to break up the sagging and zone defenses. But it was useless to talk to Buzz. He had his mind made up and, so far as Biggie was concerned, he settled everything with his parting declaration.

"Look, Biggie," he said, "I've joined up with the Independents. Coach Baxter asked me to report for practice Monday night and I'm going to do it! I'm through with the Big Reds and I'm through playing second fiddle to the great Chip Hilton!"

That was enough for Biggie Cohen. He turned away without another word and started for Speed Morris' house. Biggie was low in spirits but determined to see it through. He found Speed at home, all right, and Red Schwartz was there, too. And so was Speed's father. One look at the two Morrises and Biggie knew that old man Morris was on a rampage and that was bad news for a young man by the name of Speed Morris.

Robert "Bull" Morris was as tall as Biggie and thirty

pounds heavier. He was a cattle buyer for a big packing company and he had got his name because he could handle a side of beef as easily as most people handle a ham. He smiled a greeting when Biggie came into the room and then turned back to Speed just as if they were alone. And he proceeded to tell Speed just about what Biggie had planned to tell him.

"The first game I've seen this year and you looked like you had never played basketball. No wonder Rockwell took you out of the game. I'd have sent you home! I'm going to be home all this week and I'm going to see that game Saturday night and, believe you me, you better play the way you can play or else—" He gestured toward the door. "Now, beat it! The three of you!"

Speed was glad to get out of that house and so was Red Schwartz. Biggie was still chuckling when they turned the corner and started down Main Street. Schwartz wiped his forehead with his handkerchief. "Wow," he said grimly, "wow!"

"I'll say," Speed agreed. "When he's mad, he's mad, and today he was good and mad! Gee, I must've been terrible!"

Biggie didn't muff that chance. He agreed that Speed had been terrible, all right, and carried right on where Speed's father had left off. And he did it so well that when the three boys reached the Sugar Bowl they stopped outside long enough to grip hands and eye one another with an expression that promised bad news for Valley Falls High School's future opponents and good news for one Chip Hilton.

CHAPTER 18

STAR ON THE BENCH

THE CHIEF topic of conversation of the Valley Falls High School cafeteria customers Monday was basketball, of course. And Buzz Todd was the object of the greatest interest. Buzz had told all and sundry that he had quit the team and would play with the Independents Saturday night—"on a team where every player has a chance to score and for a coach who doesn't play favorites!"

That hadn't made too much of a hit with the Big Red "fans," but some of the students, who were disgruntled over the three defeats in a row, sided with Todd on some of the things he was saying. One or two of the Big Red regulars heard it, too, and Chip was one of these. But he had always liked Buzz, so he let it pass.

Valley Falls' veteran mentor got a surprise that afternoon. In fact, it was almost a shock. For the Big Reds tore into the practice with an eagerness and a zip which made him think of the spirit the previous year's team had shown in its drive to the championship. And that drive and pep carried over to practice on Tuesday and on the bus trip to Weston and to the game and to the victory in which Chip Hilton starred by scoring twenty-two points and making the "clutch" basket with only five seconds to play when the Big Reds were one point behind.

Rockwell was still passing up Speed Morris when he named his starting five, and that afternoon had sent Chip, Taps, Soapy, Red Schwartz and Clem Barnes out on the floor to start the game. And he had held to his guns even when Weston forged ahead and held the lead right down to the last five seconds. Rockwell knew that Morris and Buzz Todd had been close friends and he was determined to break up the individualism which had ruined the Big Reds' team play if it meant he had to lose every game.

So Speed sat it out—sat it out for thirty-two minutes and for the first time since entering Valley Falls High School sat on the bench for the entire game and watched someone else play. But he was rooting all the way and his heart leaped just as high as it could leap when Chip made that last-second stab to win the game for Valley Falls, 46 to 45.

And when the bench exploded on the court right after the gun ending the game and lit all over Chip, pounding his head and his shoulders and his back, it was Speed Morris who led the assault.

The Big Reds liked afternoon games for they could get home early and have a chance to go down to the Sugar Bowl and play them all over again. The game with Weston had been played at four o'clock in the afternoon and by six o'clock the Big Reds had snapped out of their losing streak, showered, and were in the bus singing songs and wisecracking and cheering one another as though they had won the state championship.

Soapy was standing in the front of the bus acting as master of ceremonies and leading the cheering. "All right, now," he shouted, "let's have one for Clem—"

"*Yea, Clem— Yea, Barnes— Yea, Clem Barnes!*"

Soapy applauded the cheer and then hollered, "Now, how about one for—" he twisted his head to look back at Rockwell sitting right behind the driver. Then he cupped his hands and whispered hoarsely, "Let's have one for cement head—"

The yell which followed Soapy's lead was a bit raucous, but the cheer sounded good to Rockwell.

"*Yea, Coach— Yea, Rockwell— Yea, Coach Rockwell!*"

Soapy hooked a thumb at Chet Stewart. "How about a big one for the worry wart?"

"*Yea, Chet— Yea, Stewart— Yea, Chet Stewart!*"

"How about one for the Independents?" someone shouted.

That didn't stump Soapy. "Okay, gang, let's have a big Bronx cheer!"

"How about one for the twenty-two point man?"

"*Yea, Chip— Yea, Hilton— Yea, Chip Hilton!*"

Then the gang tired of the cheering, and Soapy led the singing. Rockwell listened to the ring of the happy, young voices and his heart began to glow so much it hurt and that old lump popped up in his throat again.

"The greatest job in the world," he muttered.

Chet Stewart leaned closer. "What did you say?" he asked.

Rockwell shook his head and smiled. "I said it's good to win one! Best feeling in the world!"

The Thursday papers should have given a big play to a familiar headline "BIG REDS WIN!" but they didn't. Oh, they gave the usual report of the game and the box score, but there were no lengthy columns by Pete Kennedy and Joe Williams. No, "the greatest game in the history of basketball" was to be played in Valley Falls Saturday night and the front page, the back page, the social page, the business page, and the sports page all gave the "Independents–High School" game more space than they had given the Big Reds the year before when they won the state championship.

Sundry persons in Valley Falls made sundry wagers. Some were the ridiculous kind and some were of the serious kind. The Independents were favored by almost everyone but especially by the younger fellows like Jerry Davis. This particular group figured the game which was developing almost into a grudge contest was a good opportunity for them to renew their fight on Rockwell. They were sure that Baxter and his "modern" style of basketball would be too much for Rockwell and his out-of-date methods.

Most of the older hoop fans thought the Independents were a cinch, too, but there were a few die-hards, like John Schroeder and Bull Morris and big, happy-go-lucky Jim Rice, who believed in the kids and in Henry Rockwell.

Chip had been a three-letter man ever since he had entered high school. Now a senior, he was well on his way to making it a grand slam. He had won his letter each year either as a player or as a manager. During those years and in all the accompanying practices and games he had learned to know most of his coach's moods. But he couldn't figure out the Rockwell who was so cool and impersonal when the gang reported for Thursday's practice. He said nothing at all about the victory at Weston nor the coming Cancer Fund game.

After the limbering and warm-up drills, Rockwell worked them briefly on freezing the ball and meeting a pressing defense and then dismissed the practice. But Friday's practice found a different coach on the job. His movements were quick and his voice brittle and sharp as he sent them through the medicine ball calisthenics.

Then Chip knew that this was the Rockwell who had led the Valley Falls High School team to the championship of the state—the Rockwell who had been able to devote his time to scouting and to preparing his team to meet the attacks and the defenses they would need against the Big Reds' opponents, instead of using every minute of his time to keeping peace among his own players.

After the medicine ball calisthenics and the warm-up drill which always preceded the real work of every practice session, Rockwell waved toward the bleachers and Pop Brown rolled the blackboard over in front of the boys. Then, one by one, Rockwell wrote the names of the players who made up the starting five for the Independents and discussed each in such detail that there was amazement in the eyes of every listener.

Where had the Rock gotten all the dope? . . .

Why, he had 'em doped out to the last little detail. . . .

Say, the Rock was different. He meant business!

"Bob Dobson is the center. Naturally, in a pressing attack, there is no center, no forwards, and no guards. Every player is a forward and every player is a guard— what little guarding they do.

"A pressing attack is simply a constant advance toward the basket with little or no thought to the defense. The *pressing* principle is designed to cause you to make mistakes; mistakes like attempting a cross-court pass, or pivoting away from a teammate so they can double up on you. Keep in mind that they are constantly advancing toward their own goal. They are not interested in retreating. They don't care how many points you make just so they make one more or are one point ahead when the game is over. That's why the style of play isn't sound. That's why you're going to beat them and beat them bad!"

Rockwell paused and flashed a sharp look at each boy. There was determination in the set of his chin and Chip and every boy there knew what that meant . . . Rock was sore.

"Now back to Dobson! He's so slow he couldn't catch a cold. They use him only to grab the rebounds if you miss, or take the ball out of the net if you score. Then he's supposed to slam it up court to one of the other four fellows who drive in for the score. The sole idea is to outnumber you and drive in for the score. Lots of times Dobson is down under the opponent's basket all alone and—that's another weakness! I'll cover that later.

"Chip, you'll be playing against Dobson! And, Taps, you'll be sitting this game out. Sorry, but I know you're more interested in the team winning than you are in playing. Not that you won't get in the game! But Chip is faster and can do just what we have to do to break the back of their attack. I'll talk to you about that later, Chip.

"Pete Steup, or Porky, if you wish, is just an ordinary fat boy trying to relive high school days when he weighed a hundred forty instead of two forty! Lefty— Lefty, you'll be playing Steup. You're ten times as fast as he is and I want you to be all over him all the time.

"Bill Spotts is a pretty fair ballplayer. He's still in shape and likes to play. Schwartz, he's your problem. He goes to his right all the time and he couldn't make a left-hand shot if his life depended upon it! You'll over-shift all night on him and try to force him to go to his left! Get it?

"Hunk Moore makes all his points under the boards. He couldn't throw it in the ocean if he was ten feet from shore. That means your job, Soapy. Your job is to block him out. Block him away from the basket all night.

"That brings us to Kelly. Joe Kelly is the spearhead of the Independents attack. He is what we used to call a basket-hanger when I played ball, and that's why he makes so many points. That means one of our backcourt players will have to take him and stay with him even when we have the ball to prevent easy scores—hangers! Barnes, you play Kelly!"

Rockwell paused and, in the tight little silence which followed, every boy sitting in the bleachers got the significance of the starting line-up Rockwell had just announced.

Morris wasn't going to start . . .

Benched for two in a row . . .

Last year's captain and an All-State forward . . .

Maybe he'll quit like Buzz Todd did. . . .

Rockwell gestured to Pop Brown who had been sitting with the boys and Pop quickly cleaned the blackboard. Then Rockwell tapped the surface with the piece of chalk he still held in his hand. That was Rock's way of getting absolute attention.

"As most of you know, this team has been going to seed and I've been forced to make several changes. So far, the changes have been for the best. Frankly, I'm very happy about the spirit you have shown this week and if you keep it up you'll be the team you should have been.

"Now, benching a regular is a hard thing to do, but a coach has to make the changes he thinks are best for the team, not for the individual. Taps, here, has to ride the bench tomorrow night for a while, maybe for the whole game. But I know that Taps feels the way I do—feels that the team comes first and I'm not worried about Taps getting sore and handing in his suit, for I happen to know he's not that kind of a kid.

"Maybe some of you are wondering why I benched

Buzz Todd and Speed, here. Well, this ball club wasn't going any place, fast! I benched those two boys because all of our trouble, offensively, came from the backcourt. The backcourt players control a team's attack. Buzz and Speed forgot completely about the style of play which had been so effective and began to try to score from long range and that threw our whole scheme of attack out of gear.

"Buzz Todd, as you all know, turned in his suit and has joined up with the Independents. I'm sorry Buzz did that. I realize how tough it is to sit the bench after you've been a regular. It takes real courage to keep smiling and cheering your teammates when you know in your heart you're one of the best players on the squad.

"But there comes a time in every athlete's life when he has to bench himself through a realization of his mistakes or the coach has to do it for him. Sometimes a fellow benches himself because he forgets all about the team and gets wrapped up in himself too much. Often a fellow is sent to the side lines because of an injury or because a better man comes along. And sometimes a player has to be benched for the good of the team. That's the coach's responsibility and it's tough but it has to be done.

"Speed is one of the greatest athletes I ever coached. I don't mind saying that to his face—it's true and I'm sure he knows I feel that way about him. But Speed forgot for a little while about the team. I've been watching him for the past couple weeks and—"

Rockwell's crooked smile flashed across his face for a second and then was gone.

"And what I've seen I've liked. The athlete who stays on his toes while sitting on the bench is hard to keep off the floor!"

CHAPTER 19

TOWN VERSUS GOWN

CARS were parked in every inch of space for blocks around the Valley Falls High School gym. The parking lot beside Ohlsen Stadium was packed full and policemen were waving and telling drivers to "Keep going." People stood at the bottom of the long flight of steps leading to the gym, and two or three hundred or more were jammed against the entrance waiting for the door to open.

Chip and Soapy hurried through the side door leading to the dressing room and found they were late. Their teammates, in various suiting-up stages were yelling, slamming locker doors, and crowding over in front of Pop Brown who was issuing the game suits.

"Hiya, Chip! Hi, Soapy!"

Rockwell was standing in the corner, one foot on a chair, watching and waiting for the gang to get dressed and to be seated on the long bench which faced the rubbing table and the dressing-room blackboard. And while he stood there, his thoughts were just a little bitter. Every player, every student, and every fan and rooter in Valley Falls seemed to have forgotten the Big Reds

161

were fighting to hold their championship honors to say nothing of the leadership of Section Two.

This Independent game had even overshadowed the traditional fight with Steeltown which would take place next Wednesday. What in the world had hit all these hundreds of people? Even now they were crowding into the building, pushing, elbowing, and fighting to get in to see a high school team play a pickup team of would-be basketball players. They must be crazy. Hoop crazy! It was beyond him. But one thing was sure . . . Everyone else may have forgotten about the race for sectional and state honors, but he hadn't. Not by a long shot. He studied the faces of the kids and smiled with satisfaction. They were ready for this game all right. Ready with their plays and their fight and ready with the most important thing of all. Team spirit!

Rockwell didn't waste any time on pre-game dope tonight. He had taken care of that the evening before. When he said "Let's go" there was the usual team grip around the rubbing table and then the line formed facing the door, with Chip and the ball in the lead. Rockwell walked to the door, opened it, and away they went, crowding and stepping on the heels of the fellow in front, and pushing him just a little as you always do when you're in a hurry to "get at 'em!"

Chip pushed through the crowd which overflowed from the stands and filled the passageway leading from the dressing room to the floor and saw that the Independents were already practicing. Then when he dashed out on the floor and dribbled hard for the basket, the stands rose en masse and a roar filled the gym. These were their kids and they'd send them out fighting even though they weren't expected to win.

As Chip trotted back up the side of the court to get in line he glanced at the other bench. Baxter was stand-

ing right on the court side lines as though he were afraid
someone in that great crowd wouldn't see him. Then
Chip saw Buzz Todd taking long one-handers at the
other end of the court. It didn't seem right for Buzz to
be playing on a team against the Big Reds.

A few minutes later the referee was out in the middle
of the floor holding the ball and Chip and his starting
teammates were huddled with Rockwell for a last second "Let's go!"

Every player on the Big Reds' bench was standing up
and clapping hands and yelling and up in the stands
Mrs. Hilton stood up, too, but she was not cheering. She
just stood there with her eyes fixed on her son, the captain of the Valley Falls High School team. Mary Hilton
didn't like to go to the games in which Chip played. She
preferred to stay home and catch up on her household
chores and listen to the games on the radio. But tonight
she had given in to the wishes of Baxter and her next-
door neighbors. So here she was, standing between the
Brownings who were just as interested in their son as
she was in Chip.

Chip lined up just outside the jump circle and eyed
Dobson. Bob Dobson was six five, heavily muscled and,
just as Rockwell said, he looked slow. They shook hands
as the players of the two teams jockeyed for positions
and then the ball was in the air and Chip leaped with
the toss and the Big Reds had the ball.

The crowd cheering was one long, continuous roar as
Schwartz came in high and took the tap. Red pivoted
with the ball then and zipped it back to Chip who
landed after the tap, and then promptly lit out for the
basket. Schwartz hit Chip with a perfect pass right under the basket for an easy lay-up and the Big Reds were
out in front by two points.

The fans shrieked as they waited for the Independents famed quick-break, but nothing happened. Dobson had followed Chip too late to stop the score, but he grabbed the ball as it swished through the net and stepped out of bounds to peg a long one up court. But something was wrong. It was Chip Hilton. Chip was dancing up and down in front of him, waving his arms and kicking his feet, and, up the court, Clem Barnes was right behind Joe Kelly, while Lefty Peters was swarming all over Pete Steup. Dobson ran toward the corner still holding the ball and the referee blew his whistle to indicate that Dobson had held the ball out of bounds for more than five seconds.

Before Dobson knew what had happened, Chip wrestled the ball out of his hands, jabbed it into the referee's grip and out again, stepped out of bounds and rifled a fast pass to Lefty Peters who cut like a streak for the basket and the kids had scored again. This time Dobson didn't get the ball before it hit the floor and the official had to pick it up and hand it to him. But Chip wasn't asleep and just as Dobson caught the ball, he rushed in front of him as before, waving his hands and kicking his feet. This time Dobson was fearful of the five-second rule and he threw the ball as hard as he could toward Hunk Moore who was standing under the Independents' basket. But the ball never reached Hunk. Soapy Smith had been sticking to Moore like a leech. When he saw the long pass coming, he left him like a shot, leaped high in the air, intercepted the pass, and fired it right back to Chip.

It was a long pass, but Soapy had the wing to do it and Chip pivoted with the catch and drove into the basket for the lay-up. Dobson chased him and just as Chip released the ball he hit Chip's arm and it was a three-point play. The scoreboard flickered twice when the referee raised two fingers and then when Chip dropped the free throw through the ring it flickered again and the scoreboard showed: Home Team 7, Visitors 0.

Captain Bill Spotts called for a time-out, and the crowd-roar died down to a jumbled babble of astonishment as the fans gazed at the scoreboard in shocked surprise. The kids had scored seven points in less than two minutes.

Chip, in the huddle with the gang and Rockwell, was facing the Independents bench and he could see Baxter nodding in his direction. He looked down quickly and concentrated on Rockwell's words.

"Nice going! You're playing it just right! Don't do anything different. Just keep it up! All right, Chip? Soapy, Red? Okay, Lefty? Clem? Good! Stay right on top of them, now! Let's go!"

The Big Reds kept on top of them, all right. Not once did the famed quick-break work, and as for the long one-handers, they boomeranged because the kids rushed their older opponents every second, and the shot was more of a heave than an aimed shot. It was no contest. At the end of the quarter the Big Reds led, 13 to 5, and at the half the score was Valley Falls 26, Independents 13. Chip had scored sixteen points on six baskets and four free throws.

Rockwell was grimly proud of his kids when he followed them into the dressing room. But he followed the usual between-half procedure to the letter and then sent them back to finish the job with instructions to keep right on using the same tactics.

"Keep right on top of them, now. Give them a dose of their own medicine. They can't handle it, and they don't like it, and they can't do a thing about it!"

Rockwell was only partly right. The Independents couldn't handle it and they didn't like it, but they had decided to do something about it and that something was to give Chip Hilton the works. Joe Dobson started it right off the bat. On the jump, he leaped forward and upward and jabbed his left elbow into Chip's stomach. Only a blind man could have missed that foul. The umpire called it and Chip dropped the free throw through without touching the ring for his seventeenth point. That made the score 27 to 13.

After the free throw, Chip again prepared to rush Dobson, but Baxter had instructed Spotts to take the out-of-bounds plays. So Chip shifted over to Spotts and used the same tactics on Bill as he had used on Dobson. It worked, too, for Spotts made a bad pass which Schwartz intercepted. Red fired it back, but just as Chip reached for the ball, he was sandwiched by Dobson and Spotts with such a vicious crash that he was knocked sprawling to the floor.

Chip didn't like that play and he glanced at the Independents' bench to catch Baxter smiling and Buzz Todd and the other reserves laughing boisterously. His temper nearly got the best of him, but he fought it down and walked to the free-throw line without even waiting for the official to call the foul. But he felt better when the referee called a foul on each of his opponents and he dropped both through the hoop for his eighteenth and nineteenth points and the Big Reds led, 29 to 13.

As the game wore on and Rockwell kept the same five kids who had started for the Big Reds in there, the pace began to tell on the Independents' nerves and their tempers as well. From that time on, Chip was fouled every time he got the ball. Time and again he was elbowed, hipped, blocked, and even punched in the ribs once or twice. It was hard to keep control of his temper, but he did. He wanted to play in every minute of this game and beat Baxter and his town team as soundly as possible.

In the fourth quarter with five minutes left to play, the Big Reds led, 48 to 30. The Independents had called a time-out and it was then that Baxter sent Buzz Todd in for Kelly. Long before this, the crowd had conceded the game to the Big Reds, but in spite of the dash and fight of the kids there was a half-wish that the Independents might break loose with their rapid-fire, high-scoring attack and make the game a little closer.

During the time-out, however, someone realized that Chip Hilton had made a lot of points and that bit of news spread through the crowd and created a new interest. Then someone announced that Hilton had not made a field goal in the second half and a second later someone stated that he had converted sixteen consecutive free throws during the game.

"Nine goals and sixteen free throws! Wow!"

"That's thirty-four points!"

"The high school record's only thirty-nine!"

"Yeah, Bill Hilton, Chip's dad set that record twenty-five years ago!"

"Sure of that?"

"Bill Peters said so and he played with Bill Hilton! Played in the game with him when he made the record!"

"Joe Williams had that in his column couple months ago!"

"I heard Stan Gomez say that on the radio a couple weeks ago!"

"Five minutes left. He might tie it!"

"Point a minute? That's tough!"

"Can't do it!"

"Did it before! Scored twenty points in eight minutes against Delford!"

"I still say he can't do it!"

"Can if he gets the ball."

Mrs. Hilton heard all those remarks and all at once it dawned upon her that the reason she didn't like to go to the games was because of the memories they brought back. If only Chip could do what all these people seemed to want him to do . . . Break his father's record . . . Bill would have liked that.

When play was resumed, Buzz Todd lined up in place of Joe Kelly, and Clem Barnes, who had been playing against Kelly, extended his hand and smiled. But Todd turned abruptly away and ignored the hand. Then the ball was in play and there was a new crowd reaction. Chip didn't get it at first, but his teammates got it, all right.

"Thirty-four! Thirty-four! Thirty-four!"

Then Chip was fouled again and the cheer which went up drowned out the scorer's horn and everything except the shout which had now become a chant.

"Thirty-five! Thirty-five! Thirty-five!"

Chip was thinking about that "thirty-five" and nearly missed the toss, but it bounced around on the rim a couple of times and then dropped through for his thirty-fifth point. Then Chip got it! It was the record . . . They wanted him to break the record . . . His father's record.

"Thirty-six! Thirty-six! Thirty-six!"

Spotts grabbed the ball just as it dropped through the net and Chip chased him. But he was a second too late and Spotts hooked the ball safely across the base line to Todd. Todd pivoted smack into Barnes who had followed him and Clem tied him up.

"Thirty-six! Thirty-six! Thirty-six!"

The referee's whistle shrilled through the chant and ended the wrestling for the ball, but when he tossed it up between the two boys, Todd made no attempt to tap the ball but jumped into Barnes using the same elbow trick Dobson had used on Chip. And the referee caught it just as he had caught it before and called the foul.

"Thirty-six! Thirty-six! Thirty-six!"

"Give it to Hilton! Give Hilton the ball!"

Time was out when Barnes walked to the free-throw line and bounced the ball several times as he eyed the basket. Todd, standing at the junction of the free-throw line and the circle, said something which caused Barnes to miss the basket completely and it was the Independents' ball out of bounds.

"Give it to Hilton! Give it to Hilton! Give it to Hilton!"

Chip couldn't believe he had heard Buzz correctly, but even before Bill Spotts could get the ball out of bounds for the throw-in, Buzz said it again. And it wasn't nice. The Valley Falls captain turned toward Todd in amazement. But now the crowd was chanting again.

"Thirty-six! Thirty-six! Thirty-six!"

"Give it to Hilton! Give Hilton the ball!"

Clem followed Todd to cover him on the pass-in from out of bounds, but Todd either lost his head completely, or believed Barnes was following him in reprisal for what he had said, for he turned suddenly and struck Barnes full in the mouth. Clem staggered back and went down on one knee, hardly knowing what had happened.

Then there was pandemonium. In an instant the floor was swarming with irate fans, most of them trying to get at Barnes. Bert Todd, Buzz's father, rushed at Barnes and gave the boy a shove which nearly sent him down to the floor. Clem made no effort to protect himself but stood there holding both hands to his mouth while the blood trickled through his fingers.

Before Chip could reach Clem's side, the crowd around the boy parted as if turned aside by a giant snowplow and Bull Morris reached Clem Barnes' side and charged into action. He flayed around with his arms and fists and everyone but Bert Todd fell back. Todd was still trying to get at Barnes, but Morris grabbed him and turned him around just as easily as you spin a turnstile and shoved him clear off the court.

The Big Reds and Henry Rockwell were in action by that time and surrounded Clem as they walked back to their bench. Speed Morris had led the charge from that bench just as his father had led the foray from the bleachers. And on the floor there were Prof Rogers, Chet Stewart, and Mr. Zimmerman, the principal, and the police, and the cheerleaders, and some of the members of the band. And then, just as suddenly as it began, it was all over.

When the floor cleared, Principal Zimmerman used the loud-speaker to announce the game would continue but that it would be called off immediately if there was any recurrence of the disgraceful sportsmanship displayed by some of the spectators. The crowd cheered Zimmerman and someone started the chant again and the referee blew his whistle.

"Give it to Hilton! Give it to Hilton! Give it to Hilton!"

There was a huddle in front of the Big Reds bench, and when Speed Morris came trotting out on the floor to replace Barnes, the stocky star got a resounding cheer. And then when Clem Barnes was led away from the bench and down to the dressing room by Pop Brown and Doc Jones, you would have thought the boy had just won the heavyweight championship of the world. The crowd stood up and applauded him every step of the way and long after he had passed from sight. Then the chant was back.

"Thirty-six! Thirty-six! Thirty-six!"

The game was a mad scramble now. Just the sort of a game Speed Morris liked. He was expert at intercepting bad passes and this type of a game was right down his alley. He stole the pass-in from out of bounds right in front of the Big Reds' basket. One long step would have carried him under the hoop for a sure two-pointer, but he pivoted and burned the ball to Chip who was driving in from the corner and Chip banked it against the board for his thirty-seventh point.

"Thirty-eight! Thirty-eight! Thirty-eight!"

Spotts took the ball out of bounds, glancing at the clock as he stepped across the line. There were eleven seconds left to play and Bill used all of them he could before throwing the ball far down the court. But Soapy Smith was down there and he picked the ball out of the air and rifled it right back to Speed down by the Big Reds' basket. Again Speed faked a shot, pivoted, and bounced a perfect lead pass to Chip who had started in to follow the shot. Just as Chip took the ball and started to shoot, Bill Spotts crashed into him head on and the contact spilled them both to the floor. But the ball split the cords, and the twenty-five year record was tied.

Once again pandemonium reigned. There was so much noise that not a single person heard the official's whistle just before the buzzer sounded ending the game. In fact, players and spectators alike swarmed out on the floor in their desire to slap Chip on the back and get near the boy. But soon the frantic tooting of the referee's whistle checked them and they saw the referee leading Chip to the free-throw line.

The announcer was urging the crowd to clear the

floor under the high school basket. "Please take your seats! The game is *not* over! Hilton was fouled on that last play and has one free throw coming! Move back from the basket, *please!* Hilton has now scored thirty-nine points!"

The crowd moved away from the basket willingly enough but that was as far as they would go. It was an amazing spectacle. There must have been a thousand persons on the floor when the referee finally gave the ball to Chip for the shot and the opportunity to set a new record. It was the most difficult play in Chip's life and he had never before felt so nervous. And to make it worse the crowd took up the chant again.

"Forty! Forty! Forty! Forty!"

Mrs. Hilton and the Brownings had not moved. They had remained standing while the crowd clambered down over the seats to the floor. Mary Hilton was holding her hands over her ears to still the deafening noise, but her eyes were watching every move Chip made. But when Chip stepped to the line, arranged his feet just so, and eyed the basket, Mrs. Hilton breathed a little prayer and closed her eyes.

Chip's mother was probably the only person in that building who did not see Chip drop a perfect toss through the basket to set a new Valley Falls High School scoring record of forty points in thirty-two minutes of play.

CHAPTER 20

PLAYING IT SMART

PETEY JACKSON was in a gloomy mood the Sunday morning following the Independents game. He had opened the Sugar Bowl at eleven o'clock and here it was twelve thirty and there hadn't been a single customer. He glanced out through the front door at the driving snow which was falling so heavily that it obscured the other side of the street. What a rotten day!

It wasn't the weather which had Petey down, it was T. A. K. Baxter. Petey was thoroughly disillusioned in regard to Baxter and it wasn't because the Big Reds had defeated Baxter's Independents. Nor was it because the great man had neglected to pay for all the refreshments he had consumed at the Sugar Bowl, leaving Petey to pay the bill.

Petey was both sad and disgusted because he had believed implicitly in Baxter's long one-hand shot, the style of play he coached, and especially the stories Baxter had told about his basketball exploits up at State. All of Petey's confidence in Baxter had been swept away even before the game with the arrival of a letter Saturday morning. It was signed by Jiggs Jennings, the pub-

licity director at State, who had given Petey a complete
athletic report on T. A. K. Baxter.

*T. A. K. Baxter had played freshman basketball at
State but had never made the varsity. He had been
graduated from the University twenty-three years ago.
He had played no other sport according to the records
in the athletic department.*

It was Baxter's boastful spirit which had led Petey to
write to the University. Baxter's ego was such that he
could never be satisfied with a modest athletic achieve-
ment. He had to be the hero of hundreds of outstanding
feats. He had told Petey so many stories of his great
years as an athlete at State that Petey had thought it
would be swell to have a list of them to spring on Chip
and Biggie and Browning and some of the other guys
who didn't go for Baxter.

Petey had brooded all day about that letter. Baxter
was a faker! All those stories he had told had been lies.
Why would a grown man want to lie like that? Why
would anyone want to lie about his athletic ability?

Petey Jackson had been one of the first hoop fans in
town to buy a ticket to the Cancer Fund game. And he
had a choice seat—right behind the Independents'
bench so he could observe Baxter's bench strategy. But
after the letter came he hadn't cared much whether he
went to the game or not. But as game time approached,
his curiosity got the best of him and, when the game
started, Petey was there.

Petey muttered something and went back to staring
out the front door at the heavy snow which filled the
street and the sidewalk. He knew he ought to go out
there and sweep off that sidewalk. But he wasn't feeling up to it. He'd let it go until Soapy came to work.

Petey's thoughts went back to the game and the
things he had heard Baxter tell his players. He thought

about that for a long time and then he glanced down at the sports page he had been reading. Then the soda jerk's spirits hit rock bottom.

Even Joe Kennedy and Pete Williams admitted somewhat shamefacedly that the "wonder-shooting" bubble had burst—that Baxter's kind of basketball was fine for exhibitions and pickup games but that it wasn't championship basketball. However, both writers agreed that the experience had been good for the hoop crazy fans of Valley Falls and the Cancer Fund had benefited enormously.

Chip slept late that Sunday morning. It was nearly one o'clock when he came downstairs to find Biggie and Speed and Taps and Red Schwartz in the living room laughing and joking with his mother. It was just like old times.

Baxter made a brief appearance, stopping for a second, on his way out of the house for his "morning walk," before settling down to putting the finishing touches on "my book."

Chip was glad, for he didn't want Baxter's presence to embarrass the gang. A little later Petey showed up, announcing that Soapy was extremely lonesome and had promised to set everyone up to a "moron's ecstasy" or an "idiot's delight" if they'd come down to the Sugar Bowl and keep him company. Then Petey pulled Chip out into the kitchen to tell him "something important!"

Petey told Chip what he had observed at the game. "Chip, that Baxter guy's no good! I heard him tell the town guys to foul you every time you got the ball. He said you was a showboat and that if they fouled you a few times you'd get sore and start a fight and then the official would throw you out of the game! When he sent Buzz into the game, he told him to play Barnes rough because colored players couldn't take it! And he said a lot of other things that made me realize what a fool I've been. Why, he isn't a good sport at all!

"And, Chip, I don't know whether I ought to tell you this or not, but I got a letter from the publicity department at State and they said Baxter never played anything but freshman ball up there, and if that's true, he probably wouldn't even have known your father. Anyway, he couldn't have played on the same team with him, 'cause he was a senior when your dad was a freshman! What a liar!"

Petey was extremely bitter, but Chip made him promise not to say anything to anyone else about the letter. Later that evening, Chip busied himself down in the laboratory penning two letters—one to the Gately Pottery Company and one to the secretary of the University Alumni Association. In each, he wrote that he was very anxious to locate Mr. T. A. K. Baxter who had been graduated from the University about twenty-three or four years ago. Could he expect an early reply? It was extremely important.

Chip sat there in the basement a long time that evening thinking about Baxter and the things Petey Jackson had told him. Then he began to assemble some of the facts about Baxter which had been piling up in his mind. The water running from the tap in the sink. Why, that was one of the things he never overlooked! He always shut the water off tight. . . . It was one of the little personal tasks he never forgot. . . . And the cigarette ashes on the floor . . . And Mrs. Browning's remark about seeing Mr. Baxter coming up out of the basement several times . . . And the college picture which didn't look like Baxter . . . And the piece of pottery which had been rough and unlike the others one day and identical with them the next time he looked at it. What in the world was it all about?

On the personal side, why hadn't Baxter paid Petey Jackson? Why hadn't he paid his room rent? And if the man was such a big shot why didn't he have nice clothes and baggage?

Chip's mother called him then for a bedtime snack and he said he'd be right up. But first he made sure the water tap was shut off tight and the file locked. Then he tucked the letters carefully in his pocket and joined his mother in the kitchen.

Valley Falls got back to normal during the next three days. The town's hoop fans seemed to realize once more that the Big Reds were still state champions and still in the race for Section Two honors. Pete Williams and Joe Kennedy did a thorough job of eating crow and got back on the Big Reds' band wagon. The Independents and Baxter were barely mentioned.

Baxter had taken the licking hard. It hadn't affected his campaign to trap J. P. Ohlsen, of course, but it did shake Baxter's confidence. Baxter was the type of fellow you would call a "front runner" in sports. When everything was going smooth and breaking his way, he was fine. But when things get tough, front runners quit; they don't seem to have what it takes to fight back. Baxter was like that, too, but he wouldn't have admitted it even to himself.

The loss of the game worried Baxter, and it was, of course, a crushing blow to his personal pride. He resolved to work a little faster so he could get out of Valley Falls before things got too hot. He had learned through experience that the "hit and run" was his best play and he decided he'd have to pull off his deal as soon as possible. Of course, you couldn't rush a man like J. P. Ohlsen too fast. You had to play it smart. One little mistake in timing and the fat was in the fire. But time was running out!

CHAPTER 21

DEEP FREEZE

STEELTOWN and Valley Falls were bitter sports rivals. Year in and year out these two teams were up near the top fighting for Section Two honors in all the major sports. This year the Steelers were rugged, but the game was played in Valley Falls and the rebound from the three defeats in a row was still strong enough to give Valley Falls the edge in a closely fought battle.

Rockwell started Browning at center, Chip and Red Schwartz at the forwards, and Speed and Clem Barnes at the guards. Those five boys played the whole game. It was a bitter, hard-fought, give-and-take contest, but the Big Reds ended up on the long end of the 46–43 score. Chip was high scorer with twenty-three points and Clem Barnes was next with eleven.

That victory gave the Big Reds the lift they seemed to need. But they ran into a tartar at Northville on Friday. Rockwell had scouted Northville the Saturday after the Parkton loss and had prepared the Big Reds for Northville's "possession" game. So they were not surprised when the Northerners immediately went into their "deep freeze."

It was tantalizing basketball. Some coaches refer to

this style of play as "possession" or "percentage" basket-ball. The theory behind the style of play is based upon keeping the ball until an opponent makes a mistake and a wide-open shot is possible.

Rockwell had cautioned the Big Reds not to become anxious, not to make the mistake of lunging at the ball nor to try for an interception.

"That's what they want you to do," he warned. "So wait! Wait for them to make the first move. Make them show first. Remember, now, their whole style of play is based on the principle that their opponents can't score as long as they have the ball."

So Chip and Speed and Taps and Clem and Red waited. They waited through the first half and through the third quarter. And when the Northerners took a shot, the Big Reds jammed up the center and the sides and came out with the ball. Then they brought the ball slowly up the court and cautiously passed and passed until they had a good shot. Then they retreated and waited some more—waited until they thought they just couldn't wait any longer. But they did, smiling and talk-ing to their opponents and holding back the urge to dive at the ball, just once.

The game was close all the way. Northville would score and then the Big Reds would score. And the matching of baskets kept the Northerners in front by a single point. But time was running out. Now, with less than two minutes to go, Northville was content to play it out by holding the ball and continuing their extra-special deep-freeze attack.

Speed, watching the clock, decided to try his dummy play. Chip knew what was coming and readied his muscles to cover Speed's man if the try was unsuccess-ful. Speed had played his opponent safe for thirty min-utes. Now he played "dummy" perfectly, moving slowly and indicating in no way that he was gathering his muscles for a sudden dive at the ball. Then, just as Chip's opponent passed across court to Speed's man, the Valley Falls speedster flashed forward. His far-reaching fingers barely grazed the ball, but it was enough. The deflected ball eluded the panic-stricken clutch of Speed's opponent and, before he could turn, Speed had recovered the ball and was on his way, dribbling furiously for the basket.

Two Northerners took out in hot pursuit and Chip raced after them. And it was a good thing he did, for the taller of the two miraculously blocked Speed's shot. The ball careened off the backboard and directly above Chip's head. Chip's desperate leap carried his right hand just over the rim of the basket and he jabbed frantically at the twirling ball. It was a lucky jab. The ball bobbed back up on the rim, hung there for an instant, and then fell through the ring to put the Big Reds in the lead by a point.

The roof fell in then, but the Northville rooters lifted it right back up as they screamed for a score. The crowd hysteria gripped the Northerners then, and all the poise and assurance they had shown in handling the ball for thirty-one minutes and twenty seconds vanished. A wild, long one-hander was short and to the left of the basket, and Taps hauled the precious ball down and clutched it to his chest. Valley Falls had managed to defrost Northville's deep freeze and to win by a score of 34 to 33.

T. A. K. Baxter didn't see the Big Reds win their thrilling game from Northville, but he heard the broadcast of the game over Valley Falls own WTKO with Stan Gomez narrating direct from the scene. He heard the details of the game sitting in the Ohlsen library following dinner with J. P. and Mrs. Ohlsen.

Baxter enjoyed the evening immensely, using his glib tongue to hold his listeners enthralled by stories of his adventures in various parts of the world during his search for valuable clay deposits. Mrs. Ohlsen was visibly impressed, but Baxter was not too sure about J. P.'s reaction to his line. However, he was more than pleased with his progress because Ohlsen invited him to visit the plant and have lunch with him on the following Wednesday.

One of Baxter's special weapons, when trying to impress ladies such as Mrs. Hilton and Mrs. Ohlsen, was to use their children as the "clincher." He had made sure to learn all he could about the Ohlsens' only son, and, as the evening wore on and the basketball game brought Chip Hilton and the other Big Reds into the conversation, he cleverly maneuvered the parents into a discussion of their son, Joel.

Yes, Joel was their only son. . . . He was at Manton Military Academy where he was a senior cadet. . . . He would be home from February 27 until March 5 and they were looking forward eagerly to his return. J. P. had planned to make an important business trip earlier so that he could be with his son during the holiday.

Baxter made a mental note of the dates. It was apparent that this man and woman idolized their son, Joel. If he couldn't swing the deal before Ohlsen left on his trip, the period when the only son of the family would be home ought to be ideal. Ohlsen would be in a happy and receptive frame of mind. . . .

The following Wednesday, Baxter tried to put the "clincher" on his deal with Ohlsen before the town's leading industrialist went away. But Ohlsen was in too much of a rush, and Baxter reluctantly held up his proposition. He did lay the groundwork, however, by taking Ohlsen into his confidence and hinting at some of his findings for the making of pottery which could not be distinguished from the old Chelsea-Derby boneware. The formula for that precious pottery had been lost long ago, but he told J. P. how he had spent twenty years in developing a formula, which, if it wasn't the original, produced ware which was just as good.

"Yes, Mr. Ohlsen, I have developed a formula of just the right mixture of hard paste and bone ash!"

Baxter proceeded to discuss soapstone and feldspar and kaolin and underglazes and overglazes and soft pastes until he was holding Ohlsen in the palm of his hand. By this time it was all he could do to control himself. But he was cagey, knew from experience that delicate schemes such as this one often went on the rocks because of undue haste and poor timing. So he reluctantly restrained his eagerness.

Just before leaving and wishing Ohlsen a pleasant trip he opened his brief case and drew out a number of typed and handwritten pages. He held them in his hand a moment, assuming a worried expression on his face as if he could not make up his mind whether or not he was doing the right thing. Then, abruptly, he laid them on Ohlsen's desk.

"Mr. Ohlsen," he said trustingly, "right there on your desk are several formulas which will produce the same ware the British potters produced a hundred years ago. They aren't complete, naturally. I have to protect nearly a lifetime's work, you know. But there's enough information there to convince any chemist of their possibilities.

"It doesn't cost any more to make the old wedgwood or the old delft or the old copenhagen or the old spode than it does to make the stuff they're making in England today. These formulas right here—well, I think you will find that they speak for themselves, sir."

Baxter studied the tall, distinguished man sitting behind the desk carefully as he continued. "As you perhaps know, I am leaving for England and the Continent within the next two or three weeks to be gone for two or three years and I'd like to see these formulas and certain other ceramic discoveries I have in good American hands.

"Perhaps you are the man who should be entrusted with them. It is certain that I won't be able to devote any time to these formulas for several years, but I'd like to see the ware on its way. Suppose you look them over and we'll get together when you come back and I'll show you several pieces of ware I roughed up from those formulas. You may get the surprise of your life!

"Er, by the way, I— Guess I sound foolish, but I wish you would keep the papers locked up in your own safe and restrict them to your own hands."

J. P. Ohlsen stared down at the papers this stranger had put on his desk and in his care. Here might be the answer to the questions he and hundreds of potters had been dreaming about. If this was the McCoy, the Ohlsen pottery had the means to make the finest china in the world right here at Valley Falls. Chelsea-Derby! Old wedgwood! Majolica!

Ohlsen shook hands automatically with Baxter, almost in a daze as he watched the stranger leave his office. Then he reached for the stack of papers Baxter had left on his desk.

As he expected, Baxter and his plans made little progress for the next two weeks while Ohlsen was away, but the Big Reds made decided progress. After the Northville game, they met Hampton at home on Friday, February 7, and won by a score of 39 to 31.

Then, on the following Friday, Captain Bill Berrien and his Southerners came to town. The Southern contest was a "must" game for the Big Reds. Southern had lost but once and was leading Section Two. Valley Falls had been defeated three times. One more defeat meant that they would be out of the running. Besides, they had a grudge to settle with this team which had trounced the Big Reds on that never to be forgotten night of January 10. So they were keyed-up for the Southern game much as they had been for the game with the Independents.

Bill Berrien lined up against Chip once again, but he couldn't stop the big, blond forward this time. Chip was getting the ball now and was too clever for the rugged Southern battler. They fought it out all the way, but Chip ended up with twenty-two points to Berrien's seven. Speed and Clem (none of the Southern starting five seemed to be objecting to playing against a colored boy tonight) were bringing the ball up the floor with dazzling speed and passing it ahead to Chip and Taps. And Chip and Taps were getting the points. The Southerners fought gamely, but they couldn't cope with the fierce team fight of the Big Reds and that was the difference. Valley Falls won, 49 to 38.

Berrien left the game with half a minute to go and the two boys exchanged friendly grips. As Chip walked with him to the Southern bench, Berrien received a tremendous ovation. In some way, Berrien's gallant action in the Barnes incident at Southern had gotten around and the Valley Falls fans were happy to pay him tribute. Chip was so proud of his home townfolks, then, that he could hardly speak. But he managed to slap the Southern captain on the back and mutter, "Nice going, Bill!"

Meanwhile, Baxter was spending the most anxious two weeks of his life waiting for J. P. Ohlsen to return from his business trip. He was fretting now, and frankly worried. Was time going to upset the applecart . . . after all his careful planning?

One morning he got a bad jolt. He had slept late and

had come downstairs just as the postman was leaving the mail. He waited until the man was out of sight, and then opened the door, and took the letters and the papers out of the mailbox which was tacked by the side of the door.

Back in the living room, Baxter inspected each letter casually. Most of the mail was for Mrs. Hilton, but there were two letters for Chip. The first one was post-marked "University" and he tossed it down on the little coffee table in front of the settee. Then he saw the left-hand corner of the other envelope. It was from the Gately Pottery Company, Columbus, Ohio. Baxter's body stiffened and he inspected the envelope carefully. Then he thrust it in his pocket and started up to his room. At the landing on the stairs, he paused. He had a hunch. . . . It wouldn't do any harm to take the letter from the University along, too.

Up in his room he tore the envelopes open and his worst fears were realized. The Gately letter was from the director of the personnel department. Baxter read the words half aloud.

"No person by the name of T. A. K. Baxter is em-ployed by this company."

Baxter muttered an oath and tore open the letter from the University. He cursed again.

"We regret to advise you that T. A. K. Baxter, an alumnus of State University, to whom you referred in your letter of January 27, is deceased. Mr. Baxter was prominent in the field of chemistry and was living at his home in Padget, Indiana, at the time of his death."

Baxter had read enough. So the kid was suspicious. . . . There was no time to be lost now. He'd have to close in on Ohlsen just as soon as he returned. In the meantime, he'd have to watch the mail every day. He had known the kid was smart. . . .

CHAPTER 22

JENKINS SHOWS HIS COLORS

HOOP FEVER gripped Valley Falls again after the Steel-town game. The Big Reds played their best game of the year to win 53 to 52 with Chip leading the way on a scoring spree of thirty-two points. Now everyone was talking tournament. It was too late to win the championship of Section Two. Southern had completed its schedule with but two losses. But there was still time to come in second and duplicate last year's feat of winning the tourney up at State. Two Class A high school teams were chosen annually to represent each of the four sections of the state—eight teams out of nearly two hundred. In the Class B division, four teams were selected from each section.

Valley Falls was seething with excitement over the Big Reds' comeback. Delford and Valley Falls were running neck and neck—each with three defeats apiece. And the last game of the season for each school was scheduled for Friday, February 28, when the two tied teams would clash on the Delford court. The Big Reds were sure they could take Delford, but they followed Rockwell's game preparations to the letter.

Every day Chip had expected replies from the University and the Gately Pottery Company, but each day he had been disappointed. He gave that a lot of thought, for three weeks had gone by since he had mailed those letters. Could the replies have gone astray in the mail? Surely not both of them! Perhaps the replies had been delivered in the morning mail . . . when his mother was at work and he was at school . . . when only Baxter was at home. Perhaps Baxter, grown suspicious, had intercepted them! So, he sat down and wrote again. This time he enclosed stamped envelopes and they were addressed to him in care of the Sugar Bowl.

The days which followed were long and tiresome. Long and tiresome for everyone but T. A. K. Baxter. Baxter was putting the pressure on Ohlsen for all he was worth. J. P. had returned on Monday and he and Baxter had been closeted together in the pottery office every morning and afternoon since.

The Big Reds found practice tedious, Rockwell was irritable, and the town hoop fans were jumpy. Wednesday night Chip was in the storeroom back of the Sugar Bowl trying to whip the books when he heard a shout and the sound of backslapping. A moment later the door opened and through it came a tall, young man, dressed in a dark gray military uniform. At first Chip scarcely knew him. But then he recognized Joel Ohlsen. But what a difference.

"Fatso," Chip cried, rushing forward. Then he stopped. "I'm sorry, Joel—"

Ohlsen grinned. "Skip it, you lug," he said, extending his hand. "And don't apologize for the 'Fatso.' Now that I've lost forty pounds of blubber, I don't mind it, at all. *Used* to make me see red, though. How've you been?"

They shook hands, Chip in open admiration of young Ohlsen's "new look."

"Sure good to see you, Joel," Chip said. "You look like a million dollars!"

Joel Ohlsen smiled. "It's good to see you, too, Chip," he said with great sincerity. "I want you to know you're the first guy I looked up since I came home. I'll be over to see you tomorrow night, if you don't mind. It will be like the old days. I'd like to see your mother, too. How about me dropping over about seven thirty?"

"Swell, Joel," Chip said. "Mother'll be glad to see you."

"Okay, it's a date!" Joel flecked an imaginary speck of dust off his coat sleeve and then grinned. "How do you like the rig? I'll wear a real dressy getup tomorrow night, just for your mother. So long!"

Joel Ohlsen arrived at the Hiltons' the next evening promptly at seven thirty. He was wearing another fancy rig, too. Baxter was just leaving as Joel arrived and they exchanged quick glances and a nod, but neither spoke. After Mary Hilton had greeted Joel and departed hurriedly to fetch a piece of her newest cake and a glass of milk, Joel asked Chip about Baxter.

"He live here? Baxter?"

Chip was surprised. "You know him?" he asked. "Sure, he lives here, all right. He's our star boarder!"

"I don't know him," Joel said slowly, studying Chip, "but Dad knows him. You don't like him!" he said flatly.

Chip assured Joel that he wasn't particularly fond of Baxter but added nothing more.

"I don't like his looks, either," Joel said darkly, "and I'd like to know what he and the old man are cooking up. He was out at the office yesterday with five or six pieces of pottery and he and the old man puttered around with them all afternoon."

Chip was startled but concealed his perturbation as best he could and quickly changed the subject. As soon as Joel left he hurried down to the cellar. His hands were shaking as he unlocked the door to the lab and hurried to the table where he had placed the five pieces of pottery. He examined each piece carefully. Gosh, these weren't his father's work. Now they all felt like that one piece had felt that other time. They were imitations!

He sat down on the stool by the file and tried to figure it out. If this wasn't his dad's pottery, then someone had put five imitations in the lab in place of the original pieces of ware. Why? And if someone had put these imitations in the lab that someone must have been Baxter. It had to be Baxter! Mrs. Browning had seen Baxter coming up out of the basement. . . . Baxter smoked cigarettes. . . . That would account for the ashes. . . . The running water was proof someone had been there. . . . The five original pieces were gone and five imitations had taken their place. . . . Why? Joel said Baxter had five or six pieces of pottery at the office when he talked to J. P.

He snapped his fingers. That was it! He'd go see J. P. and sort of sound him out about the five pieces of pottery. Better yet, he'd take the imitations with him. He'd drop around to see Joel Sunday morning and just accidentally see J. P. at the same time. Maybe Baxter was planning some kind of joke on him. After all, how had Baxter, or whoever it was, gotten into the lab? The door hadn't been damaged. And he knew he hadn't left it open or unlocked. That was the one thing he was *always* careful to check. . . .

Chip was so busy with school and getting things done ahead of schedule at the Sugar Bowl so he could make the trip to Delford that he didn't have time to think much more about Baxter. That night one of the worst storms in years hit Valley Falls and almost paralyzed the little town. Bus lines were crippled and it was impossible to drive a car. School was a farce. Students were late, cold, and out of sorts. But storm or no storm, every student had but one thought in mind—the game with Delford that night.

Rockwell took a look at the deep snow and immediately canceled the bus. Then, just before the eleven o'clock class change, one of the P.A. announcements stated that the basketball squad would leave on the journey to Delford by train instead of by bus and the team members were to assemble in the gym at twelve o'clock sharp so there would be ample time to catch the Mainliner at one o'clock.

Speed, sitting across the room, turned and shook his head resignedly and Chip knew exactly what he meant. The trip to Delford by train took three hours and was anything but pleasant under the best of weather conditions. With the deep snow and the change at Valley Junction it would be a most uncomfortable trip. And uncomfortable it was! The through train which they were supposed to take at one o'clock was late, and they arrived at the Junction at two thirty instead of two o'clock. They were delayed for an hour, finally pulling out on the Evening Express which consisted of two freight cars, a mail car, a milk car, one antiquated day coach, and a caboose.

The storm grew worse as they went north and at five o'clock it was snowing so hard you couldn't see out of the windows. But that wasn't the worst of it. The fireman of the engine, which was to pull the Evening Express, had left his cab to get a hot dinner at his home near by, when the station agent had reported the Mainliner to be late. So the steam pressure had gone down and the dirty day coach, with its red plush seats, was stone-cold. And it got colder. There were only a dozen or so passengers on the train, traveling salesmen, Stan Gomez of WTKO, and several farm women with little tots and babes in arms. The women and the older men complained bitterly to the conductor and his train crew, but there was nothing they could do. Soapy tried to rise to the occasion by calling the others' attention to a hole in one of the windows.

"This car was the last word back in 'sixty-one. Look, here's where one of the Rebels' bullets hit!"

But Soapy's effort fell flat and soon the coach was quiet except for the crying of the children. The fireman never did get a full head of steam in the battered old engine, and the snow was piling up on the track. The train made stop after stop. Each time it was harder to get under way again. At last when they were still three miles from Delford, their destination, they stopped for good.

The conductor announced that the snowplow they had been following had broken down and that they would have to wait until it was repaired. Rockwell asked how long he thought that would take and he replied, "One guess is as good as another, but I figure not less than two hours."

"Two hours!" Rockwell repeated, turning to Prof Rogers. "That's no good! It's six o'clock now! What'll we do, Prof?"

Rogers cast a worried glance at the boys. Each one was huddled up in his seat, crowding as close as possible to his seatmate. Chip and one or two others had covered the children with their overcoats and the expressions on their faces indicated they were half frozen.

"Maybe we ought to hike it, Hank," Rogers said.

Rockwell asked the conductor if there was a road near by and if he thought it would be open. The conductor shook his head emphatically. "I wouldn't try it," he said, "it's a mile away and I doubt if they've been able to get through. If you're going to walk it, I'd advise you to stay right on the track!"

The other passengers decided that they might as well freeze trying to get somewhere as freeze sitting still, and so they all piled out of the day coach and strung out in a long line to plod through the deep snow, heads bent against the stinging blizzard. There was some skylarking in the beginning, but as they found it increasingly difficult to breathe in the face of the gale, they soon became silent, taking turns in breaking the path.

Chip, Speed, Soapy, and Red Schwartz each carried one of the little tots. It was rough going and, although the others spelled them off from time to time, they were fighting for every step and every breath before they had gone a hundred yards.

It was seven thirty when the Valley Falls basketball team lined up at the desk of Delford's leading hotel. They were so dog-tired they could hardly move. Chip wanted only one thing, a bed—and lots of time to spend in it.

"Get the boys to their rooms right away, Chet," Rockwell ordered. "I'll call Jenkins and see if we can't postpone the game until tomorrow."

Stewart and Rogers exchanged glances. They knew that Rockwell would rather eat powdered glass than ask a favor of Jenkins.

"When that cheap skate hears what shape we're in after battling through the snow," Chet observed bitterly, "you can bet your last shirt he'll insist on playing tonight!"

Chet was right. Jenkins disavowed any responsibility for the storm, said that the officials were already at the high school, and that the crowd was beginning to come and that Delford wasn't the only place where it snowed.

How about his boys? They'd been battling the snow, too. Furthermore, just because Rockwell and his jerks had won the state championship last year gave them no right to try to run all the basketball schedules in the state. His team would be ready to play at eight thirty and he'd demand that the officials forfeit the game to Delford if Rockwell and his delicate little hothouse boys didn't show up.

When Chip and the gang heard that they were up in arms. If that was the way Delford wanted it, they could have it that way! The Big Reds weren't running out on any game as long as they could stand on their feet.

The game was played. Only a corporal's guard was there for an audience and Rockwell chalked up another little mark in his long score against Jinx Jenkins for that lie. The officials were there all right, and they agreed that according to the rules Jenkins was right about the forfeiture.

The game was sheer murder. Each team was geared up to a high pitch, and, although the Big Reds were so tired they could scarcely move, they were full of fight. Chip's legs and arms felt numb, not with the cold, but with such a feeling of fatigue that he felt as though every move was being made by some other body than his own. Taps Browning got a cramp and had to be carried off the floor, writhing in pain. Red Schwartz and Clem Barnes were down and out, but managed to play a pretty good first half. But in the second half, they faded with every minute. If it hadn't been for Chip and Speed and Soapy the game would have been a massacre.

Chip and Speed played their hearts out. Red Henry and his teammates played hard, too, for this game meant an invitation to the University for the state championships. They played to win, but they gave every indication that they sympathized with the plight of their opponents. Strangely enough, the slim crowd of Delford rooters cheered for the Valley Falls team more than they did for their own. The word had got around that Jenkins was forcing these dead-game kids to play when they were hardly able to stand up, and the fans, what few there were, booed Jenkins every time he made a move. But that was small consolation for a little group of sick, tired, and broken-spirited kids who were playing on sheer nerve just to prove they were good sports. Only the fighting leadership of Chip and the burning anger of Speed and Soapy kept the Big Reds in the ball game and it even looked for a time as though that fight and that leadership were going to win.

Delford led at the half, 24 to 18. But in the second half, Chip took charge of the scoring and picked up twenty-four points practically all by himself. He was hot, and the rest of the Big Reds followed Rockwell's instructions and gave him the ball every time they came down the court. With less than ten seconds to play, the Big Reds were in front, 47 to 46, and it was Delford's ball. They swept down the court desperately trying for that last, good shot. And Chip and Speed and Soapy and Bill English and Red Schwartz were giving their last bit of energy to hold on to that slim one-point lead. Then it happened!

A Delford guard tried a wild, hope-heave set shot with two seconds left to play. Every player, coach, official, and spectator followed the flight of that ball. And every eye gauged its flight correctly. It was too long, it might go clear over the backboard. The Delford players groaned. Then the crowd uttered a long-drawn-out gasp of astonishment as the ball seemed almost to stop in its flight. Then it seemed to zigzag through the air and, as it did, it changed its arc and headed straight for the basket.

The exultant shout which had broken from the Big Reds changed to dismay as they saw the ball dropping toward the ring as though it were being pulled by a string. Down the ball fell, in an ever and ever steeper arc and then it came to rest, in fact seemed to droop, over the six-inch arm which separates the ring from the backboard.

The Big Reds stood motionless, mouths open, gaping at the ball coming to rest there on the very edge of the basket like a setting hen. And while they looked at it in amazement, the air kept rushing out of the ball until it was fully deflated.

At the very instant the deflated ball hit the arm of the basket a tall form shot forward. Chip, who had hazarded a quick look at the clock, shouted a warning to Bill English, but Delford's Red Henry already had leaped high in the air to tap the deflated ball through the ring just as the buzzer sounded ending the game.

Chip flashed an agonized look at the referee who was holding up his hand with two fingers extended to denote a score and Chip's dismayed eyes saw the electric scoreboard blink twice and then register Delford 48, Valley Falls 47.

Pandemonium broke loose! Rockwell was on the floor arguing with the officials for all he was worth and Jinx Jenkins was waving a rule book and shouting at the top of his voice that the basket counted. And that was the way it had to be. After a long argument and repeated reference to the rule book, Rockwell was finally convinced that the officials and Jinx Jenkins were right. But it was the final straw in a day and an evening of mishaps, disappointments, and heartbreaks for the Big Reds.

CHAPTER 23

HOME TOWN RALLY

MRS. HILTON had her hands full at the telephone exchange the next morning with another storm. But this storm had nothing to do with the elements. It was a storm of a personal nature, brought about partly because the Big Reds had lost at Delford, but chiefly because of the spellbinding wizardry of Valley Falls' own WTKO sports expert, Stan Gomez.

Gomez had made the trip to Delford on the train with the Big Reds, and he had seen Chip and the other kids give their coats to the women and children and sit shivering through the long, cold ride from Valley Junction. Then he had stumbled and slipped and waded and fought his way through the heavy snow and the bitter winter night, marveling at the gallantry of the boys in the straggling line up ahead, as they struggled through the snow, breaking a path and carrying the little tots in their arms. And he had realized that these kids were unselfishly expending their energy and game strength to help those who needed help so badly.

Later, ace reporter that he was, Gomez had caught the significance of Jenkins' dirty trick, and the reaction of the Delford players to the extremes to which their coach would go to win. And Gomez had caught something more. He had caught the antipathy of the hoop-crazed Delford fans to Jenkins' poor sportsmanship.

All that Gomez had observed, and heard, and the way he felt about it himself, was sufficient to fire him with a fervor of speech which came from the heart and which thrilled every man, woman, and child who listened to his broadcast. Just about everyone in Valley Falls was listening that bitter winter evening, and just about everyone in Delford who wasn't at the game was listening, and never before did a sports announcer have such a sympathetic audience. Before the game was over many thousands of fireside listeners knew that they had been hearing not only a stirring account of a nerve-tingling basketball game, but one of the most dramatic stories of unconscious heroism, on the part of a little band of high school kids that had ever been told on the air.

The Delford people wasted no time in starting to do something about the way they felt. They got busy on their telephones that night and early the next morning and the fuss they made led to an emergency meeting of the Delford Board of Education and the prompt dismissal of Jinx Jenkins, a man who should have never been in charge of kids, anyway. A telegram was sent addressed to Carl L. Zimmerman, principal of the Valley Falls High School, stating that Delford High School didn't want to win games or championships or invitations to tournaments that way and that they would like to replay the game.

So sincere and so inspiring were Stan Gomez's words that everyone in Valley Falls forgot all about the outcome of the game and the end of their tournament hopes and everything but the fact that the kids who carried their colors in competition with high school kids throughout the state were too big to shirk a duty and a gallant deed even though it meant the loss of their chance at the state championship.

But Rockwell and Rogers and Stewart and Chip and his teammates knew nothing about all this. Coming back on the train the next day, they were steeped in despair and defeat, and sick in body, some of them, and sick at heart, all of them.

At the Junction, some of the boys bought papers and Chip caught a glimpse of the headline on the sports page. It was something about Southern and Delford, but he was too tired to care much about it and he dozed off again. Most of the boys felt just as Chip did, too tired and worn out to care much about who had been selected to take part in the tournament. Taps and Clem were both running a fever and anxious to get home.

As the train neared Valley Falls, Chip and all the kids began to think how difficult it was going to be to face the townfolks. Chip looked out the window and couldn't help thinking how tough it was going to be tonight at the Sugar Bowl, and he wished he didn't have to work. And then he began to think about Baxter, but somehow or other he didn't much seem to care what the man was up to. He was just too doggoned bone-tired to care about anything now. Finally he closed his eyes again and tried to rest.

But now the train was passing Morrisville and the brickyard and the pottery and suddenly they were slowing down for the Valley Falls depot. Chip, awakening from his doze, thought he heard the sound of music. He thought, at first, someone must have a portable radio on the train, but then the tune began to register and it was the Valley Falls Victory March. The tired boy shook his head and felt sure that he was imagining things. But the music grew stronger and, like everyone else, he peered out the window to see where the music was coming from on this gray winter day.

Then he saw the band—the red-and-white capes, with the boys in white trousers and the girls in their white skirts—and they *were* playing the Victory March! And he saw Dink Davis and the cheering squad and the whole platform filled with kids and men and women who were all cheering and yelling and waving banners. Chip simply couldn't figure what it was all about.

The train stopped with a little bump and the hissing of air brakes. Rockwell led the way through the aisle and down the steps with his shoulders squared and his chin up and they all followed with Chip the last to make the platform.

Right then, you would have thought the President of the United States had come to visit Valley Falls. Chip had never heard such cheering as his teammates and he were being hustled through the crowd which surged closer and closer along the platform until they came to two baggage trucks. Mr. Zimmerman, the principal, was standing up there and he was smiling and applauding just like everyone else. Still Chip didn't know what it was all about. Then the Big Reds found themselves being hoisted up on the trucks and Mr. Zimmerman was trying vainly to check the great cheer which again went up. And then suddenly everyone was quiet.

Mr. Zimmerman was beginning to speak. As though from a great distance, Chip heard the principal telling Rockwell and the team how proud the people of Valley Falls were of their sportsmanship and their fight and the way they had acted and played at Delford. There was a lot more to it and Chip didn't hear it all, but he heard enough to realize that the people of Valley Falls may have been hoop crazy but they weren't quitters. . . .

They didn't quit on their kids and their coach just because they had lost. Then, as Zimmerman talked, and the crowd cheered the things he said, all the heartache and all the tightness in Chip's throat, and the bitterness and the hurt feeling which had swelled his chest, were gone. Chip looked at the gang and their eyes were bright now, and some were smiling, and Rockwell's mouth was slanted into that crooked smile and all of the despair of the Big Reds seemed suddenly to have vanished. It was as though a storm which had been raging suddenly had quieted and left nothing behind but clean streets and a new, clear and sunny day.

It wasn't so bad that afternoon at the Sugar Bowl, after all. Petey and John Schroeder and Doc Jones and everyone were cheerful, saying they'd had their share of championships and "Wait until next year!"

Later, Petey brought two letters back to the storeroom and dropped them on the desk one at a time. "There's your scholarship from State, Chipper," he said, grinning cheerfully, "and here's a letter from a pottery company. Probably want the formula for that pottery you sold at the exhibit."

Chip's heart jumped.

He thanked the soda clerk and tossed the letters carelessly on the desk. But as soon as Petey had left he tore them open. The first letter was from State and it was a copy of their original letter. They were sorry it had failed to arrive. It had probably been lost in the mail.

"We regret to advise you that T. A. K. Baxter, an alumnus of State University, to whom you referred in your letter of January 27, is deceased. He—"

The second was from the Gately Pottery Company and it, too, said this was a copy of their original letter which must have been lost in the mail.

"No person by the name of T. A. K. Baxter is employed by this company!"

Chip sat there a long time studying the letters and turning their significance over in his mind again and again. So Baxter was a faker . . . Assuming someone else's name . . . Had lied about being an executive in the Gately Company . . .

Anyway, that settled it . . . There was something wrong. . . . Tomorrow he'd see J. P. Ohlsen and tell him the whole story.

Saturday nights were big nights at the Sugar Bowl. All dates managed to make that stop before or after shows, and this night was no exception. Chip, Soapy, and Petey were kept busy all evening, and the three were ready to call it a day when Speed thoughtfully arrived at close-up time to drive them home.

Chip was dead-tired, but he couldn't get to sleep. He hadn't seen Baxter since he had come home but his mother had told him that the man had been working awfully hard out at the pottery with J. P. Ohlsen.

"He's been out at the pottery every night, Chip. He was out there tonight! His book is finished, by the way, and he sails for England, I believe, next week."

Baxter was up early the next morning and out of the house before Chip got downstairs. After breakfast, Chip read the papers. The sports pages were concerned chiefly with the Delford game and the letter from the Delford principal offering to replay the game. And Chip read again what Joe Kennedy and Pete Williams had written in Saturday's papers.

"Valley Falls High School appreciated the spirit and sportsmanship which prompted the offer to replay the game, but all concerned agreed that a game once played and lost couldn't be re-won. So as far as the Big Reds and Coach Rockwell and the students and the Valley Falls basketball fans were concerned, Delford had earned the right to their invitation to the tournament."

It was a slow, dull morning; that is until Soapy and Speed and Red and Biggie arrived. Then, perhaps because Chip was dreading the interview with J. P. Ohlsen, the time seemed to fly. The gang talked over the game and the reception the home folks had given them and the tournament and the probable winner. But Chip was preoccupied and his friends sensed that he had something on his mind and that he wanted to be alone to work it out, so they left after a while. Unable to think of any other excuse for delay, Chip started out for Ohlsen's. As he approached the house on the hill, he remembered a previous visit to this home. He always seemed to be in a jam when he called on his father's old boss.

Joel Ohlsen was on the butler's heels when the door opened. Joel had been in the library and had seen Chip walking up the long drive.

"Hiya, Chipper. What you doin' up here this time of day?"

"Why, just fooling around, Joel. Except that I wanted to see your father for a couple of minutes."

"He's not home, Chip. He's down at the office. Important?"

Chip nodded. "It's important to me, Joel. I've got to see him—today!"

Joel smiled. "That's easy! He's down at the plant. Wait till I get my car and I'll drive you down."

Chip started to protest but Joel checked him. "Won't take but a sec. Come on! I'll drop you by the gate. You don't mind if I rush back? Got to take Mother some place."

Joel dropped Chip at the gate to the pottery and Chip walked over to the office building entrance which was located a short distance beyond the employees' entrance gate. He tried the main door but it was locked. He walked over to the little side entrance where the Sunday watchman, Sam McQueen, was on guard.

McQueen knew Chip and grinned as he stopped by the open check window. "Where do you think you're going, young fellow?" he asked.

"I'd like to see Mr. Ohlsen, if he's not too busy."

"Well, he's busy, all right! Fact is, he's so busy he left strict orders no one was to be admitted. Got DeWitt the chief chemist up there and a feller by the name of Baxter. Been up there all morning—doin' some kind of special work. Anyway, he said he didn't want to be disturbed! Told me not even to come up and check the office!"

"But I've just got to see him," Chip insisted.

McQueen shook his head decisively. "I'm sorry, Chip, but I can't let you in. If it's awfully important, why don't you wait over there on the other side of the door by the wall? He can't stay in there forever."

McQueen closed the window and then locked the steel gate which led to the main yard. "Well," he said cheerily, "I hope you get to see him. I've got to make my rounds, now. Sorry I couldn't let you in, Chipper, but you know how it is— Orders is orders! So long!"

Chip leaned against the stone wall by the office door and resigned himself to a long wait. And it was a long wait. The hours dragged slowly by and his feet were cold and he kicked the toes of his shoes against the wall to keep the circulation going and he got hungry and the tired feeling which had gripped him during the past few days returned, but he waited. Twice, McQueen, on his rounds, stopped to speak to Chip, and went away again shaking his head. At last, at six o'clock, Marty DeWitt, Ohlsen's chief chemist, and T. A. K. Baxter came out of the building and walked briskly away through the evening dusk.

Chip had started when the door opened, but when he saw who it was, he stood quietly by the wall as DeWitt and Baxter passed by a few feet away. He thought Baxter's eyes flickered sideways in his direction, but he couldn't be sure.

As soon as they were out of sight, Chip knocked on the panel and was rewarded, at last, when Ohlsen heard him and unlocked the door.

"Why, hello, Chip, what are you doing here?"

"Why, I'd like to talk to you about something important, Mr. Ohlsen."

"That's fine, Chip, but I'm awfully busy right now. If it isn't urgent, I'd rather talk to you tomorrow."

"But it is urgent, Mr. Ohlsen. It's about Mr. Baxter!"

"Baxter? What about Baxter? Here, come into my office. Now, sit down and tell me what's bothering you about Mr. Baxter."

"Well, Mr. Ohlsen, I guess maybe I shouldn't be telling you this and maybe it's not as important as I think it is, but— Well, sir, I don't think Mr. Baxter is Mr. Baxter— I mean, well, here's a letter I got from the Gately Pottery Company that he claims he worked for and here's another from the University, and they— Well, sir, you read them."

Ohlsen was alert now, and his hands trembled just a little as he grasped the letter. As he read, he gradually pushed the letters further and further away across the desk, as if he didn't want to believe the words. When he finished reading the two letters, his eyes were disturbed and there was a worried look on his face.

"What prompted you to write to State and Gately, Chip?"

Chip told him about the picture which did not resemble the stranger, and about the basement laboratory and his suspicions with respect to Baxter's integrity when Petey had showed him the letter he had received from the University. Then he told how Baxter had acted on the bench in the Cancer Fund game and how that had made him so sore that he had written the letters. And he told Ohlsen about the peculiar changes in the five little pieces of pottery.

Ohlsen now was sitting bolt upright in his chair. When Chip had finished, he walked over to the safe and brought out a cardboard box and took out five pieces of pottery which Chip recognized immediately as his father's work.

"Are these the pieces?" Ohlsen asked, his voice tense with emotion.

"Yes, sir, they sure look like them. If they're not Dad's they're exact duplicates!"

"And you're sure there are five pieces of pottery in your cellar lab right now?" Ohlsen demanded.

"Well, sir, they were there when I left the house this afternoon."

Ohlsen turned away from his desk and began to stride nervously back and forth across the office. His brow was wrinkled and Chip could see that he was deeply moved. He turned back to Chip once more.

"Chip," he said searchingly, "are you sure these are the same size and shape as the ones in your basement lab? Are you positive?"

Chip nodded. "Yes, sir! Identical!"

It was evident to Chip that J. P. was laboring under terrific emotion now, for his voice was sharp and the words almost tumbled one over the other as he spoke.

"Chip, I want you to go right home and bring those pieces of ware you have in your cellar over here! And another thing! Bring along a few of your father's formulas. And don't say a word to a soul about this, not even your mother. Hurry!"

CHAPTER 24

MR. BAXTER FOULS OUT

When Baxter stepped out of the pottery office building, the quick, side glance which Chip had caught was comprehensive even though it was cleverly concealed. DeWitt hadn't noticed Chip at all, but Baxter saw him and his confidence suddenly was shattered. This venture had been right on the verge of success. In fact, he had sold Ohlsen completely. But now something told him that there were breakers ahead.

When DeWitt turned off three blocks away from the pottery, Baxter made sure he was out of sight, and then hastily retraced his steps. It was just about dark now and his footsteps made no sound as he hurried along the snow-covered street. Across from the pottery office he stopped in the shadow of an old building and watched the light in Ohlsen's office with anxious eyes. Although he couldn't see Chip and didn't know whether he was in the office or not, he could see Ohlsen striding back and forth and he didn't dare leave. He had to know whether or not Chip Hilton was in that office, and if he was, he had to know what he and Ohlsen were talking about. What was that kid doing down here, anyway?

His patience was rewarded a few minutes later when

Chip emerged from the building and hurried away. Baxter followed at a safe distance, but when Chip started to jog along the slippery streets, he had difficulty keeping pace. However, he was close enough to see Chip enter the Hilton house and see the light flash on in the basement a few seconds later. Then Baxter's anxiety almost got the better of his prudence. If only he could see what the kid was doing in that basement.

Chip was doing exactly what Baxter was worrying about, wrapping newspapers around the five pieces of pottery and placing them in a small basket. He had already opened the filing cabinet and taken out several bundles of his father's formulas. Fortunately, Mary Hilton was upstairs. Chip had entered the house quietly and tiptoed down the cellar steps without disturbing her. Now, he made his way quietly out of the house and started back to the pottery office.

Baxter saw the basket and he knew the worst. And when he saw Chip making his way swiftly back over the same route which he had just traversed from the pottery, Baxter knew for a certainty that the jig was up. Young Hilton had put Ohlsen wise to something.

The letters he had intercepted had been the tip-off. The kid had been suspicious all along and something must have happened in the last day or two to confirm his suspicions. What to do? Beat it? How could he? Where could he go? He didn't have a cent. Leave now with thousands of dollars almost in his grasp?

Then Baxter thought of the large brown envelope in the safe in Ohlsen's office and he suddenly broke into a trot and turned to his right. At the first alley he turned left and sprinted as hard as he could go toward the pottery. He had to pass that kid and beat him to the office.

Short of the building he stopped in the shadow of a small alley and while he waited he fitted the heavy key case in his right hand and thumped his left several times. Baxter had always prided himself upon his cleverness and his ability to get out of ticklish situations without the use of a dangerous weapon. He smiled grimly as he felt that heavy hardness. Then he pulled his belt from around his waist and rolled it up and placed it in his coat pocket.

Chip came along the street, close to the fence, deep in his thoughts of Baxter and this pottery mystery. That was the reason he saw only a swiftly moving shadow. He ducked instinctively but not soon enough and Baxter's key-enforced fist crashed flush on the side of his jaw. The vicious blow staggered the boy and, even as he fell, Baxter struck him again. This time the blow landed at the base of the skull, and Chip fell heavily to the walk, out like a light. The basket he had been carrying dropped from his hand and was lost in the snow.

Baxter glanced to right and left and then dragged Chip quickly into the shadow of the fence in the alley. He pulled his belt out of his pocket and strapped Chip's hands behind his back. Making the gag was more difficult, but he fashioned one out of his handkerchief and thrust it into Chip's mouth and tied it firmly back of his head. Baxter was cruel in this task as the hatred for this kid welled up in his heart. He thumped Chip's head roughly against the snow-covered ground and then rolled the boy over against the fence, before hurrying toward Ohlsen's office.

J. P. Ohlsen was a careful man and under normal circumstances would have checked the door to his office when Chip hurried away. But the sudden change in events had left him confused and disappointed. After Chip hurried out of the office and down the long hall to the door to the street, Ohlsen sat down wearily in his chair and tried to figure how he had permitted himself to be tricked by this glib-talking stranger. He shook his head and muttered bitter self-denunciations for having permitted himself to be made the fall guy of such a cheap confidence man. Why, even Joel wouldn't have been taken in by such a farfetched scheme. He groaned as he remembered how he had rushed to swallow this shabby trickster's bait, hook, line, and sinker. If word of this ever got out among his ceramics associates he'd be the laughingstock of everyone in the trade.

While Ohlsen was sitting there berating himself, Baxter gently opened the outside door and crept softly along the hall and up the stairs. When he reached the half-open door of Ohlsen's office he paused and got his bearings. He had to make sure that the watchman was not in the building. His right hand was bunched menacingly in his coat pocket as he gently pushed the door open with his left hand and stepped into the office. Ohlsen was so deep in thought that he never even turned his head.

"Come in, Chip," he said absent-mindedly, "put them over here on the desk."

Then he glanced up and saw Baxter standing in the door. He was bewildered for a moment and he arose angrily to his feet. "You—"

Baxter's pocketed hand jerked upward and he moved menacingly forward. "No, *you*, Ohlsen. You! Now just sit back in that chair and keep your mouth shut or I may have to close it forever."

Baxter's eyes shifted toward the safe and back to Ohlsen and a smirk of satisfaction stole across his lips. "Good," he said with satisfaction, "the safe is still open! I was afraid I might have to force you to give me the combination! There is no reason why we shouldn't complete our little deal right now instead of waiting. I happen to be in more of a hurry than I thought."

Keeping his hand in his pocket he moved quickly to Ohlsen's desk. Then he stepped behind Ohlsen and swiftly tied his arms to the back of the desk chair.

Ohlsen didn't move, but his eyes were burning with anger. "You'll never get away with this, Baxter," he said through tight lips. "Never!"

Baxter's response was a brutal slap with the back of his hand against Ohlsen's mouth. "Shut your trap, Ohlsen," he rasped, "and keep it shut! I mean business! Now when I call your house I want you to tell your butler to send your car down here on the double. Tell him to park it in front of the building and give me the keys and then to go on home because we'll probably be working all night. Get it? You'd better! Because when that car gets here, you and I and a nosy kid by the name of Chip Hilton are going on a ride! No, not the kind of a ride you're thinking—not unless you try to get out of hand! We're men of the world, Mr. Ohlsen, and I imagine you are not going to be too anxious to let people know what a fall guy the great J. P. Ohlsen turned out to be."

Baxter dialed the Ohlsen residence and held the speaker to Ohlsen's mouth. Then, just as Baxter had directed, Ohlsen ordered his butler to send the car down to the office immediately and to give the keys to Mr. Baxter who would meet him in front of the building.

Baxter smiled with satisfaction as he cradled the hand phone. "Very good, Mr. J. P. Ohlsen," he said smoothly, "very good! Now, I'll have to have expense money, naturally, for my trip to England and I'd better get busy and get it! You just sit quiet and everything will be hotsy-totsy!"

Baxter swung the door to the safe wide so he could

watch Ohlsen as he began systematically to go through its contents. He tossed the papers and other contents carelessly on the floor. One little door inside the safe was locked and Baxter smiled sarcastically as he pulled the packet of keys out of his pocket. He'd take care of that, pronto.

Meanwhile, Chip was struggling to get his head above water. But every time he got it above the surface, a grinning-faced Baxter reached a long hand down and pushed it back under. But Chip kept struggling. The water was ice cold and he knew he was going to freeze if he didn't drown, as he kept redoubling his efforts to reach the surface and make his way ashore. Gradually his senses returned, and he was dumbfounded when he realized that his hands were tied behind his back and his face was jammed deep down in the snow and he wasn't in the water at all. . . .

Then his mind clicked back to the events which had happened just before Baxter had shoved him into the river. Now he knew that there hadn't been any river at all but that there had been a Baxter and that it had to be Baxter who had slugged him.

Suddenly he remembered J. P. Ohlsen waiting for him in the office. It seemed years ago that he had left it to go home to fetch the fake ceramics to show J. P. Violently he wrenched at the belt to get his hands free. When he finally got them loose, he started painfully to get to his feet. He got only as far as one knee when he felt as though Baxter had struck him again. But it wasn't Baxter this time, it was just a sharp, piercing pain in the back of his head which nearly dropped him off into un-consciousness again. Unthinkingly he did the right thing by grasping a handful of snow and holding it to the back of his head.

It took an almost superhuman effort to get to his feet and he staggered once or twice and fell over against the fence as he looked up and down the street. But it was a factory street and there were no friendly lighted house windows to give him his bearings. Then Chip caught sight of the lights in Ohlsen's office and he started in that direction, weaving a bit but gradually regaining his strength and his wits.

Chip was surprised to find the outside door unlocked when he tried the knob, but he pushed it open. When he got inside it was so quiet he was scared. Maybe something had happened to Mr. Ohlsen. . . .

He slipped quietly up the steps and then he heard a rustling noise and through the open office door he saw Baxter at the safe. He tiptoed softly forward and then he saw Ohlsen tied to the chair. J. P. saw him at the same time and shook his head warningly, whispering in an effort to tell Chip to go for help. But Chip kept moving on toward Baxter. Then Baxter's "sixth" sense warned him and he swung around.

"Watch out, Chip," Ohlsen shouted, "he has a gun!"

But Chip wasn't watching out for anything. He only knew that T. A. K. Baxter, or whoever he was, had caused him a lot of trouble and had slugged him and that he now appeared to be robbing J. P. Ohlsen's safe. He hurled himself across the room at the crouched figure of Baxter, and Ohlsen was horrified to see Baxter's hand come out of his pocket. But then Ohlsen was surprised to see that it wasn't a gun which Baxter held at all, but a short piece of wood.

Chip didn't see anything except the smirking face of the man he despised and whom he now saw unmasked for the criminal he really was. Chip hadn't fully recovered, but he was fired by an intense hatred and that added fury to his attack. He smashed head on into Baxter in a clumsy body block and they went down in a heap, struggling desperately as they threshed about on the floor. Baxter knew all the dirty little tricks and he had the advantage of superior height and reach, but they seemed to have no effect upon the aroused youngster.

While they fought, Ohlsen was shouting for help and he struggled so hard to free himself that he and the chair tumbled to the floor, and there they were, all three wrestling and straining and battling on the office rug when Sam McQueen dashed breathlessly into the room.

McQueen had heard the noise from the foot of the stairs and had come running, but he had never expected to see the sight that greeted his eyes. Before he could grasp the situation, Baxter was up on his feet and dashing for the door. McQueen started to swing his watchman's clock at Baxter, but it wasn't necessary. Chip launched himself in one desperate flying tackle at Baxter's heels and the two tall figures crashed into McQueen and then he was on the floor, too. All he accomplished was to catch one of Baxter's flailing blows on the right ear.

Chip was on top now and McQueen heard Ohlsen shouting that one Sam McQueen would be out of a job if he didn't untie his hands right away. So Sam crawled over the chair and over the writhing forms of Chip and Baxter and succeeded in loosening Ohlsen's hands. Then he crawled over to help Chip hold a frenzied confidence man on the floor while Ohlsen called the police.

Later, after the police had driven away with Baxter in a squad car, Ohlsen leaned back in his chair and held his head. And on the other side of the desk, Chip Hilton leaned forward and held his head. The dour expression on the other's face moved each to a grin, sickly as it was, and then Ohlsen got up and went to the safe. When he came back he was holding a large brown envelope and he told Chip to open it. Chip opened the envelope and saw more money than he had ever seen in his life.

Ohlsen was watching the surprised expression on the face of the boy and he smiled at Chip's astonishment. "Yes, Chip, twenty-five thousand dollars, and he'd have had it all the first thing in the morning if it hadn't been for you."

"You see, Chip," Ohlsen continued, "Marty DeWitt and I both fell for his formulas because the ware there on the desk—your father's ware—is wonderful stuff. But it's the clay content of those pieces of ware which sold me. Of course, I didn't know that until tonight. I thought it was the formula which was responsible for the beautiful work.

"Today we can't get that kind of clay in quantity and that was what Baxter counted on— He was clever enough to know that it was the clay which was responsible for the ware and not the formulas, so he substituted the imitation pieces and brought the real pieces here as specimens.

"Baxter was smart with respect to his money deal, too. He wanted to sell the formulas for cash only. Said he wouldn't have time to arrange a bank deposit, for he had closed all his accounts and wanted to use the cash to invest in foreign markets and, presumably, his plane-booking tomorrow out of Chicago and then New York would not permit him time to cash a check.

"Everything was all set for tomorrow here in my office at eight o'clock when he was to deliver the complete formulas, sign the receipt for the money you have there, and catch The Chief at nine o'clock for Chicago.

"Yes, you saved me twenty-five thousand dollars and from being the laughingstock of the entire pottery trade. I want you to know that I appreciate all you have done to spoil Baxter's devilishly clever plan to fleece me by means of your father's research and experiments. We both realize, Chip, that money can't pay for a service such as you have performed."

Ohlsen counted out ten one-hundred-dollar bills and placed them in Chip's hands. "I'd appreciate it, son, if you would add this to that college fund."

"I couldn't, Mr. Ohlsen— I didn't do anything— Why, my mother wouldn't stand for it!"

Ohlsen's smile was understanding as he took the money from Chip's outstretched hands.

"All right, Chipper," he said gently, "I'll talk to your mother about it, tomorrow— She and I understand each other. There are supposed to be a good many ways of skinning a cat. There must be several ways of adding to a smart boy's college fund, too. Now run along and have Mary Hilton put a cold compress on that noodle of yours. You're going to need it when you get up to State!"

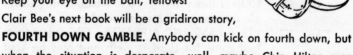

Keep your eye on the ball, fellows!

Clair Bee's next book will be a gridiron story,

FOURTH DOWN GAMBLE. Anybody can kick on fourth down, but when the situation is desperate—well, maybe Chip Hilton was justified in calling the play he did! Read all about it in **FOURTH DOWN GAMBLE.**

Your Score Card–
of CLAIR BEE'S Famous
CHIP HILTON SPORTS STORIES

Your local Bookseller has all of these books!